Edmund Hodgson Yates

The Impending Sword

A novel

Edmund Hodgson Yates

The Impending Sword
A novel

ISBN/EAN: 9783337213527

Printed in Europe, USA, Canada, Australia, Japan

Cover: Foto ©Andreas Hilbeck / pixelio.de

More available books at **www.hansebooks.com**

THE

IMPENDING SWORD.

A Novel.

BY

EDMUND YATES,

AUTHOR OF 'BLACK SHEEP,' 'THE ROCK AHEAD,' 'THE YELLOW FLAG,'
ETC. ETC.

'Put we our quarrel to the will of Heaven,
Who, when He sees the hours ripe on earth,
Will rain hot vengeance on the offenders' heads.'
SHAKESPEARE.

IN THREE VOLUMES.

VOL. I.

LONDON:
TINSLEY BROTHERS, 8 CATHERINE ST. STRAND.
1874.

CONTENTS OF VOL. I.

Book the First.

THE EMPIRE CITY.

Book the First.

THE EMPIRE CITY.

VOL. I.

CHAPTER I.

THE CURTAIN RISES.

'AND you really insist upon my going?'

'Insist is not the word. Stay here if you like it better, and amuse yourself by drinking brandy-and-soda-water, which, since your visit to Europe, it seems you cannot do without. All I say is, that I shall go, and if you want to see some pretty women you had better come with me.'

'What did you say the man's name was? and where does he live?'

'His name is Griswold—Alston E. Griswold—and he lives in Fifth-avenue, just above Thirty-sixth-street. He runs a bank, and is all day long in Wall-street, and makes a pile of money, they say. He ought to, for he lives in elegant style.'

'And his wife—he has a wife, I suppose
—what is she like? Does she come from
New England and sing through her nose, or
from out West and drawl like—'

'What stuff you are talking, Redmond!
Since you have come back from Europe
there is no bearing with you. Why don't
you go back to the other side and get yourself made a prince, or a duke, or something?'

'Ay, why don't I? Why, because—however, that is none of your business. Is Mrs.
Griswold pretty?'

'Very pretty and excellent style, and
always has the nicest people in New York
in her house.   Let us go and see them;'
and the speaker rose from the chair which
he was occupying in front of one of the
fireplaces of the reading-room of the Union
Club, pitching away the butt-end of his
cigar and pulling himself together as though
preparing for a start.

'Wait a minute,' said his friend, yawning lazily; 'I don't like leaving this fire, it is so confoundedly cold outside.'

'Cold, nonsense; you have got that hideous Ulster coat which you brought from England, and there are plenty of robes in the coupé. We shall not be five minutes spinning up to Griswold's, and once there, you will be very glad you came.'

So the two young men, Redmond Dillon and Charles Vanderlip, went out into the hall of the club and wrapped themselves up in their overcoats, and were whirled away up Fifth-avenue as hard as Vanderlip's wiry little horses could lay their feet to the ground.

Charles Vanderlip was right in saying that his friend Alston Griswold was very rich, for there were evidences of his wealth and of the lavish manner in which he spent it before his door was reached. Although it was early spring, traces of the severe winter yet remained in huge masses of snow piled up into a high dirty frozen heap,

which extended along either side of the
avenue, with interstices cut here and there
to allow of access to the house; but within
twenty yards of either side of Mr. Griswold's
house these icy barriers had been levelled
and carted away, a broad canvas-covered
passage had been made from the inner door
to the outer edge of the side-walk, and no
sooner was the outside barrier passed than
you immediately merged from cold and
dreary darkness into warmth and light, into
an atmosphere heavy with perfume from
the innumerable flowering shrubs with
which the rooms, the passages, and the
staircases were decorated ; into a species of
fairyland, where the ears were greeted with
the sound of enlivening dance-music exqui-
sitely performed, and the eyes were delighted with the sight of the prettiest
women in the world in such perfect toilettes
as the most lavish expenditure could pro-
cure.

'This man really does the thing very

well indeed,' said Dillon to Vanderlip, as they made their way down the staircase towards the parlour where the reception was being held.

'Does he, indeed? How very kind of you to patronise him!' said his friend with a laugh. 'Why don't you pull your moustache, Redmond, and say "Haw" to every word, after the true English swell fashion? Wait until I have presented you to Griswold and you have talked to him, and then you will find out what a true gentleman and thoroughly good fellow he is.'

They had gained the door now, and were being carried on with the tide of humanity that was surging through the room; the crowd was great and almost constantly in motion, but as the host and hostess stopped every one to say a few kindly words of recognition as they passed the mantelpiece, which might in military language be called the saluting point, Redmond Dillon had plenty of time to take a good

look at Mr. and Mrs. Alston Griswold before his presentation to them.

A man of about six-and-thirty years of
age was Alston Griswold, of middle height,
with a thick dark moustache and a small
imperial, bright, frank, honest dark eyes,
and a gentlemanly, intelligent, good-looking
face. A few lines here and there round his
eyes tell of business cares, and his shoulders are slightly rounded from frequent
stooping over his desk. For this night,
however, he had temporarily abandoned all
thought of business care or worry. You
would have thought him the least preoccupied man in the world, if you had noticed
the gay courtesy with which he addressed
each of his guests as they passed by; you
would have thought him the best man in
the world, had you chanced to mark the
glance of mingled pride, love, and admiration which from time to time he threw
upon his wife, standing by his side.

Nor could he have bestowed upon her

any amount of admiration or affection which would not have been richly deserved, for Helen Griswold was a woman among a thousand. Rather under than over the ordinary height of women, with a figure which, though light and lithe, was rounded and shapely, with perfect little hands and feet, and with a gliding walk, such as is rarely seen save among Spanish women, for one of whom she might have passed. Her eyes were large, soft, and dark, her complexion creamy, her hair the very darkest shade of brown, shot here and there with a tinge of deep dull red. Add to this a small straight nose and a rather large fresh mouth, and you have Helen Griswold's portrait complete.

By this time the two club men were abreast of their host and hostess, to whom Vanderlip presented his friend as just returned after a long absence in Europe. Helen merely bowed and smiled, but her husband shook hands with Dillon, and

laughingly congratulated him on safely ac-
complishing a voyage which he himself was
about to undertake.

'What did he mean by that?' asked Dillon of his friend when they had passed
through the crowd and were standing in
the further room, where dancing was going
on. 'You don't mean to say he is going
to Europe?'

'I imagine so by what he said; indeed,
I recollect now hearing at the club he sails
in the Calabria to-morrow, and that this
is a kind of farewell fête.'

'Of course he takes his wife with
him?'

'I think not. She would give the world
to go, but is encumbered by the ties of ma-
ternity. Her little baby is delicate, and the
mother could neither take her nor go away
from her.'

'Isn't Griswold fond of his wife?' asked
Dillon, looking through the arched opening
between the rooms at the host and hostess,

who, having finished their reception, were now approaching the dancers.

'Fond of her! He worships the ground she treads; you have only to look at them to tell that.'

'What makes him leave her, then?'

'Business, my dear fellow, to which, as you appear to have forgotten, all the men in New York are slaves. Griswold is deeply interested, amongst other matters, in the establishment of some new telegraphic line which is to compete with the Western Union, and rumour reports that his present mission is in search of English capitalists and English engineers to aid him.'

'And he leaves his wife behind!' said Dillon, shaking his head. 'Poor child! I thought by the expression of her face that there was something clouding her happiness even to-night.'

'Yes; in these days, when conjugal fidelity is somewhat at a discount, their devotion to each other is extraordinary. I never—'

'Say, quick, who is this man leaning against the wall with his arms folded, and looking so intently at Mrs. Griswold?'

Vanderlip looked round in the direction pointed out. His eyes rested on a tall man, of slim but wiry build, about twenty-eight years of age, with a long, thin, close-shaved face, small deeply-set eyes, and thin blood-less lips. His evening dress was scrupu-lously plain and neat, and as he leant back against the wall with his legs crossed, one hand was hidden in his bosom, while with the other, long and lean, he slowly stroked his chin. His gaze was fixed, and never varied; its object, as Dillon had remarked, was Mrs. Griswold.

'That,' said Vanderlip, after looking at him, 'is a man of some importance in this household. His name is Trenton Warren, and he is perhaps Griswold's most intimate friend. He is a clear-headed 'cute fellow, versed in all the mysteries of "bulling" and "bearing," and is supposed to be Griswold's adviser in all matters of business, and the real mainspring and contriver of these lucky hits by which his fortune has been made. Trenton Warren is supposed to be quite necessary to Griswold's existence.'

'And from the way in which he looks at her apparently seems to think the contemplation of Mrs. Griswold necessary to his own,' said Dillon. 'He hasn't moved his eyes from her since she came into the room.'

'You never were more mistaken in your life, my good friend,' said Vanderlip, with a smile. 'Perhaps the sole fault of Warren in Griswold's eyes is that he cannot be brought to admire Mrs. Griswold sufficiently; that he does not give her credit for the rare qualities which her husband and his other friends believe her to possess.'

'Do you mean to tell me, then,' asked Dillon, 'that that man is not reckoned among Mrs. Griswold's admirers—I mean

of course admirers in the proper sense, of
whom you may be considered one?'

'Certainly not! It is said that he was
averse to his friend's marriage with the
lady, and that he has always entertained
somewhat of a dislike for her since.'

'Didn't approve of the marriage? Ah,
perhaps he wanted her for himself?'

'Bah! Trenton Warren is the last man
in the world to whom such an insinuation
could apply. He thinks of business and
nothing else, and is so singularly apathetic
about Mrs. Griswold's grace, beauty, and
good qualities, as really to rile and vex her
husband, who wishes all the world to be as
cognisant of them as he is himself.'

'What a large-hearted man!' said Dillon,
with a cynical smile. 'And so I am entirely wrong about Mr. Trenton Warren,
am I?' he added to himself, as Vanderlip
moved off to speak to some ladies. 'And
he has no admiration for Mrs. Griswold?
Well, I am not usually wrong in such mat-

ters, and as I have nothing else to do until
Vanderlip is ready to go, I may as well
amuse myself by watching what is going
on around me.'

Let us take advantage of this opportunity to sketch a little of the previous history,
and to describe the relations then existing
between Helen and Alston Griswold and
Trenton Warren, three personages who are
to play most important parts in our drama.
And first let us see that Redmond Dillon,
clever by nature and sharpened by experience, was not very far wrong in his judgment of the actual position of affairs. All
that he had heard from Vanderlip about
Trenton Warren was correct. The one annoyance of Alston Griswold's life (out of
his business career, which, as is usually the
case, was full of annoyances) was, that his
friend· could never be prevailed upon to
speak, as her husband thought, sufficiently
warmly of Helen.

And yet if all had only been known, Warren's appreciation of the woman at whom he was then gazing, with all his soul glowing in his eyes, was really greater than that bestowed upon her by her husband. Alston Griswold thought his wife the prettiest, dearest little creature in the world—one on whom it was impossible to bestow too great an amount of petting and affection, one whom it would have been impossible for him to deceive or betray—far beyond any other woman in the world, but still a woman, and as such inferior to man; something to be caressed and petted and spoiled, a pretty plaything, a charming solace for one's leisure hours, but nothing more. Alston Griswold would have scouted the idea of talking over any affairs of vital importance with his wife, of making her the confidante of his business schemes, of asking her advice in regard to any detail of the great struggles in which he was constantly engaged ; she would not have understood them, he thought, and why should she be bored with them ?

Trenton Warren knows her better than this. His sense is far finer, his insight far keener, than his friend's, and while he has apparently stood aloof from any attempt at intimate acquaintance with Helen, and has been sufficiently sparing of her praises in her husband's ears, he has brought all his sense and keenness to bear upon the dissection of her character, and has arrived at a far different estimate of her mental power. Constant secret study of her tells him that, if she is not exactly clever, she has an immense fund of common sense, determination, and patience—tells him also another thing, the thought of which sends the blood into his pale cheeks, and causes his heart to throb with exultation. Helen Griswold, this pattern wife, so decorous, so much respected, so universally looked up to, holds her husband in highest esteem, in most affectionate appreciation, but of love for him —of love, be it understood, in the sense of passion — she has, according to Warren's idea, not one whit. Such love the placid easy-going absorbed man of business—so much her elder too, with his petting parental way—was not one to kindle ; and yet such love, if Warren were any judge, was as necessary to her as air to light or heat to flame. He had watched her carefully, and he read the necessity for it in the occasional wearied expression which came across the lustrous depths of her dark eyes, in a certain unsatisfied restlessness which from time to time she betrayed; he imagined he had discovered her craving for love of a distinct kind from that which her husband bestowed on her, and in this discovery he found hopes for his own future success.

For this man, outwardly cold, self-possessed, and reticent, so far as Helen Griswold was concerned, was the slave of a passion, violent, unreasonable, unconquerable. He struggled against it for a time, fearing the probable trouble, the danger it would cause him; and when finally he found resistance to it impossible he determined that by her alone should its existence be known. All his apparent insensibility to Helen's charms, all his studied depreciation of Griswold's enthusiasm about his wife, were caused by what he felt to be the imperative necessity of keeping his passion hidden until the time should arrive for declaring it to its object, and to her alone.

And Helen—what was the state of her feelings towards Trenton Warren? She could scarcely have told you if you had asked her. But in her secret self she knew that she regarded him with dislike, almost approaching to loathing, without being able to account to herself for the detestation he inspired. She was afraid of him without any definite cause for her fear, suspicious without being able to explain to herself the reason for her suspicions. That he has any tender feeling, any of the animal passion which men of his stamp dignify by the name of love, she does not dream for a moment.

Had such an idea crossed her mind, her dislike of him would have been intensified. It was on her husband's account that she first conceived this distrust of Warren, who, she felt certain, was exercising an evil influence over Griswold, and worming himself for a bad purpose into her husband's confidence.

Helen had this conviction so strongly that it would have been impossible to dispossess her mind of it; and yet, feeling as she did the difficulty of reasoning it out to herself, she saw clearly the utter impossibility of making her husband understand it. Even if she could have explained herself, she doubted very much whether she could have carried conviction to Alston's mind; for Helen's keen and accurate judgment had long since taught her to comprehend the exact manner in which her husband appreciated her, and to know that, though most kind and loving and admiring, he regarded her merely as a sweet solace for his hours of relaxation, and would have certainly misunderstood anything she might have said to him in regard to Trenton Warren, and imputed it to a womanish jealousy of his male friends.

What was it that filled Helen's mind with these reflections at a time when she ought to have been thinking either of the gay scene around her, or of the loneliness which would fall upon her on the morrow, when her husband should be gone? What was it that set her speculating upon the motives which could possibly prompt Trenton Warren to be so assiduous in his attention to her husband, so desirous to conciliate him and to secure his intimacy and confidence? What was it? She was answered at once, as she raised her eyes and saw the man who had occupied her thoughts standing immediately opposite, his gaze bent full upon her!

Was Trenton Warren taken off his guard? Had the sight of the woman for whom he had entertained so fierce a passion —sitting there radiant in youth and beauty, her full evening toilette contrasting some-

what strangely with her air of preoccupation, almost of sadness—caused him for an
instant to drop the mask?   Or did he think
the time had come when the revelation of
that passion might in safety be made? Certainly, there was an expression in his eyes
such as Helen had never seen there before
—an expression which caused her to drop
her own instantly in amazement and indignation.

The next moment he was by her side.

'It is strange to see you sitting here
alone, Mrs. Griswold,' he said, with a slight
tremor in his voice, which, however, he immediately got the better of ; 'and you are
generally so surrounded as to make ap-
proach to you impossible.'

Helen did not look up at him, but there
was nothing in his tone or his words to
which she could take exception; so she
merely said :

'It is surely not from experience that
you say that, Mr. Warren.   Your apprecia-

tion of my society has, I imagine, never been so great as to induce you to take any trouble to enjoy it.'

She was looking straight before her, and the expression of her face was deadly cold; but the words spoken in her musical voice fell deliciously on Warren's ear.

'But it is never too late to mend,' he said, 'we are told by our schoolbooks and by Mr. Charles Reade. If my shortcoming has been so great I will hasten at once to repair it. They have just started a waltz, you are not engaged, will you give it to me?'

He bent over her so closely that she felt his warm breath on her hair. Drawing back hurriedly, she again saw the expression she had already noticed in his eyes.

'Thank you,' she said, with great coldness; 'I have no intention of dancing.'

Her frigid decided tone must have struck him, for he looked at her with surprise, and said,

'You cannot be tired, Mrs. Griswold?'

'Since you say so, of course I cannot,' she replied, looking him full in the face; 'for what you say, at least in this house, Mr. Warren, is not to be contradicted; nevertheless, I will take upon myself the risk of declining to dance and of holding to my word.'

Trenton Warren looked as though he would have spoken, but Helen, by a slight bow and by an almost imperceptible movement of her hand, gave him to understand that the interview was at an end.

'The horror with which that man inspires me increases daily,' she said to herself, as he moved slowly away; 'but never have I seen him so odious, so offensive as just now. I dread his intimacy with Alston, not merely on account of the influence which it may have on our fortune, but from some undefined dread that he will work mischief between my husband and myself. See him now even at this instant.   He makes his way to Alston's side, and by the expression of Alston's face, and the way in which he looks towards me, I can tell as certainly as though I were at his elbow what he is saying. He is speaking of me kindly, and lovingly too, I am sure; in the confidence of his friendship he is commenting on my appearance to Trenton Warren. How blind he is! Can he not detect the contemptuous sneer with which his friend is listening to him? The very look which I saw in his face the other day when he complimented me on the possession of that rare treasure, "a husband who admires his wife and is not ashamed to say so." No, Alston sees nothing of that, and still continues to— Mr. Warren takes his leave. Ah, thank Heaven, there is a general move! I am tired and out of spirits, and shall be only too delighted to get rid of all these people.'

Trenton Warren accepted one of the numerous offers to him of conveyance to

his house; but although it was sufficiently late when he reached home, and he
knew that the next morning he must be up
betimes, having much important business
on hand, he did not think of going to bed,
but throwing himself on a couch, lit a cigar,
and became absorbed in contemplation.

'She hates me,' he muttered, after a
pause, slowly expelling a cloud of smoke;
'and after her treatment of me to-night, I
declare I almost hate her. I hate her for
her coldness; the way in which she constantly avoids me, and for her calm insol-
ence when compelled to acknowledge my
presence. What makes her shun me so, I
wonder? Is her avoidance of me caused by
fear, arising from dislike, or is it the vague
sense of displeasure with which a woman
regards a man who has found out—while
she meant to keep him at the greatest distance—that her feeling for her husband,
though very pure and very gentle, is but a
milk-and-water feeling after all, without a

trace of passion in it? No matter much which it may be, I shall soon find out. I read somewhere recently that the first thing to be done by a man who is courting a woman is to make her think about him, even though it be unpleasantly. So far, I imagine I have succeeded with Helen Griswold; she cannot keep me out of her thoughts just now, even though she think of me with dislike and fear.'

Having arrived at which satisfactory conclusion, Mr. Trenton Warren pitched away his cigar and went to bed.

CHAPTER II.

'GOOD-NIGHT' and 'good-bye.' These words, uttered by Alston Griswold to certain departing guests as he stood on the top of what is called in New York the stoop (equivalent to our steps) outside his open door, gave a fresh turn to the last proceedings of the evening. Good-bye? Why, of course, he was going to Europe the next day; most of them had forgotten that, and many of them thought it a favourable opportunity for cracking another bottle of champagne to wish their host health, happiness, and a safe voyage. Those wishes for the prosperity of others, which always increase in fervour with the advance of the night and the circulation of the wine, were mingled with the expression of hopes from some that Griswold would not remain away long; that he was a representative New Yorker, one of their merchant princes, and a thoroughly good fellow, and of fears from others lest when he did come back he should be spoiled and Europeanised, as was the case with too many of them; but none of these expressions of doubt were whispered above the speaker's breath, while all the good-byes and God-speeds were loud and protracted, so that a man of less genial and kindly impulses than Alston Griswold might have been excused in indulging in a little self-gratification at the esteem in which he was held, and the regrets of losing him which were so loudly manifested.

The last guest had gone, and Griswold, after waving his farewell to them from the door, had turned back into the hall, when it suddenly struck him that his wife had not been present at these final joyous ceremonies. To stand well in her eyes, to have her as the mute witness of the honours paid him in acknowledgment of his social and commercial position, was his greatest pride, and he was vexed and angry to think that the warm compliments of which he had just been the recipient had been unheard by her.

He looked into the supper-room, but she was not there; into the ball-room, and there he found her on a seat at the far end, listless and dejected.

'Helen, what ails you?'

And all his anger vanished in an instant as she lifted up her eyes, and he saw they were filled with tears.

'Helen, my darling, what is the matter? Has anything happened?'

'Nothing, dear,' she said, in a low flat voice. 'Tell me, are the people all gone? every one, I mean? O, I am so glad!'

'You are over-fatigued, child, that is all,' said he, bending tenderly down to her.

'I wish it were all,' said Helen, rising

and throwing herself into her husband's arms. 'I am so horribly wretched!'

'Wretched!' he repeated, with infinite tenderness. 'What makes you wretched, dear?'

'You do, and no one else. You are going to leave me, and it seems cruel and unkind of you.'

'My sweet Helen, those are very hard words, and—'

'I don't mean them harshly, Alston; but you have no idea how I dread your absence. If I have any influence with you, you will give up these plans and stay with me.'

'Put off my voyage now, on the very eve of my departure, with all my plans arranged? It would be impossible, Helen.'

'Nothing is impossible to you in business if you choose, Alston,' she replied; 'but you don't choose. You are carried away by the inordinate ambition to be rich. That contemptible money-worship, which is everywhere sapping the foundations of New York society, has you for one of its high-priests, and my comfort and my happiness are nothing in comparison with your desire for the accumulation of money.'

Griswold was silent for a moment, regarding her earnestly; then he pushed his hair from off his forehead, and with the faintest sigh and a grave smile, more in his eyes than on his lips, said,

'You are speaking hurriedly and like a woman, Helen, and do not, I am sure, mean half you say; but even if I have this wild desire for the accumulation of money, for whose sake is it indulged in, to whom is the acquired wealth devoted? Not, I think—' and a grave smile now broke on to his lips —'not, I think, to myself entirely. I go down town in the morning in the stage for ten cents, and I return on foot; my clothes are the standing topic for my friends' abuse and—'

'I know, Alston—I know it all. You are the least selfish of men; and it is for me and for my sake alone that you are condemning yourself to a life of slavery, and making both of us wretched. But this is precisely the reason why I am the person to enjoin you to give it up. We are quite rich enough for my ambition, dear. Stay with me, and let us enjoy together what we have. But for Heaven's sake do not leave me.'

'I love to hear you talk like this,' said he, putting his arm around her as she pillowed her head on his broad chest and looked up with soft entreaty into his face. 'It shows you to me as what I have always known you to be, the most affectionate and most trusting of God's creatures. But though I would give my life to save you a pang, what you now ask me is an impossibility. If I had had any idea that you would have taken my going away so much to heart, I would have endeavoured, though it would have been difficult, to send some one else in my place. At this late hour, however, it is impossible to make any such substitution, and it is imperative that I should go in person; not merely to look after my own business, but after very large interests of others, which have been staked on a guarantee that I would attend to them. Helen, darling, when you say that my inordinate ambition to be rich and my worship of money are greater than my love for you, you talk foolishly, and you know it. To part from you will half break my heart. I would willingly surrender all the profits, large though we expect them to be, of this projected undertaking, if by so doing I could remain with you; but I could not do so without a sacrifice of honour and credit; and, utterly unbusinesslike as you are, you know the meaning of those two words and the value which is necessarily attached to them. Do you understand me, child?'

'Yes,' she said, wiping the traces of tears from her face and looking up at him almost calmly, 'I understand all you say, and I see there is nothing for me to do but to acquiesce in the arrangement. Only understand one thing, Alston; this protest of mine against your leaving me is not the mere pettish fancy of a woman who hates to be alone, or who is possessed by any absurd jealousy as to what may be her husband's proceedings during his absence—you and I understand each other too well for any nonsense of that sort; but I hate you going away on this voyage, Alston. I have had a presentiment about it which nothing can dispel, though which I should find impossible to explain. However, it is useless saying any more about it; only promise me one thing, that you will never undertake such a voyage again.'

'I promise; that is to say, I promise never to sail again for Europe unless you go with me. O, you need not purse your little mouth up in that manner! Charley Vanderlip tells me that his friend Dillon, who has just returned from the other side, vows that Europe is the only place in the world fit to live in.'

'Then Mr. Dillon is a—never mind; I will say not a good American citizen,' said Helen, tossing her head. 'Do you know what o'clock it is, Alston?'

'Late enough,' said Alston, looking at his watch; 'but I have some work to do in the library before I can think of rest.'

'I will join you there, then,' said Hélen, rising. 'I am not in the least sleepy, only I must first get rid of this stiff silk dress, and these bracelets and jewels. I can then send that wretched Hortense to bed, and I will be down again in five minutes.'

Alston Griswold leaned back in his chair, and looked long and lovingly at his wife as she glided away, and at the spot which she had occupied after she had passed out of his sight. Then his brow darkened, and he thrust his hands deeply into his pockets as he slowly rose from his seat.

Did he share the presentiment as to his departure which his wife had confessed? Not the least in the world. He was by far too practical a man of business to have given way to any such folly. But the word —and yet— No, it would be madness. He would be the laughing-stock of Wall-street and the butt of his clubs if he allowed a woman's weakness to influence him in a matter where three or four millions were involved, and in the conduct of which his reputation and his fortune would be made or marred. He would close up his preparations at once, and the first thing to be attended to was that letter of instructions.

Acting at once upon this determination, he crossed the hall and entered the library —an old room furnished with black oak, and entirely surrounded with antique bookcases filled with a choice collection, which, indeed, their owner never opened, but which were Helen's greatest resource and delight. On the other side of the large open folding-

doors were the supper-rooms, the lights in
which were still burning, though the tables
had been cleared ere the servants retired to
rest.   Griswold looked somewhat surprised
when he saw the room still lighted, and
was on the point of ringing the bell; but
remembering there was no one to answer
it, he turned back into the library, lit a
cigar, and seating himself at the writing-
table, took from one of the drawers a sheet
of paper, two sides of which were already
covered.

By the shaded light of the kerosene
lamp, which stood upon the writing-table,
Griswold read this paper carefully through;
then laying it down before him, fell into
a train of thought. 'It looks innocent
enough,' he said; 'it might be what I shall
tell her it is, when I put into her hand—a
mere paper on business, to be read at a
future time—and yet to think how all-
powerful it will be, or ought to be, in the
event of anything happening to me.   To

be read at some future time, eh! I think I
can see the scene which will occur at that
future time plainly enough; what a com-
motion there would be in Wall-street, what
an anxiety amongst a certain set to know
whether I had carried out the commission
with which I had been intrusted, before I
died. The commission with which I have
been intrusted, that is what they would be
anxious about—not me, their agent; only
poor Helen would think of me. What she
said just now about her little regard for
wealth was true enough. If the enterprise
succeeded, she would be rich as an empress;
if it failed, she would have comparatively
little to live upon ; but in neither case
would she care much, I flatter myself, if I
were gone. The joys or the woes of life
would affect her equally little if I were not
there to share them with her. What a
wretchedly gloomy train of thought I have
fallen into!' he muttered, half aloud, striking his hand upon the desk. 'Hundreds of

men go to and return from Europe every
week ; it is the boast of the Cunard Company that they have never lost a passenger,
and yet here am I, in rude health and
strength, picturing to myself what is to
happen after my immediately approaching
death.   Helen must have innoculated me
with a touch of her presentiment; however,
I will shake it off at once.   I will finish this
letter of instructions, for it is better for her
in any contingency to know exactly how
she stands, and then I will get some rest, of
which I fancy I am more than usually in
need.'

He drew the paper towards him again,
and bending over the desk commenced
writing earnestly.   From time to time he
paused in his occupation and stared earnestly before him, as though weighing certain matters in his mind before committing
his thoughts to paper.   At length, after
about ten minutes' work, he came to the
end of his task ; and, having folded the

letter, placed it into an envelope, and was about to return it to the drawer, when he suddenly stopped.

'No,' he muttered ; 'in her present state of mind it is best to be prudent over such a matter as this. I will not leave it behind for her and tell her where it is; I will not give it to her myself, for she is but a woman, and her woman's curiosity might impel her to open it at once, and that would certainly impose a scene between us; I will send it to her to-morrow by Warren. Helen will not come down to the wharf; Warren is sure to be there to see me off, and I will send the letter to her by him. I have only him to trust to for seeing after her while I am away, and this little commission will break the ice between them, and show her to him—though he has never properly valued her—in colours that must compel him to acknowledge her the perfect wife she is.'

So saying, he sealed the letter and

deposited it in his pocket-book, after restoring which to his breast he continued his musing.

'What a wonderful stroke of luck for me, situated as I am, to have made such a friend as Trenton Warren! He will be indispensable to Helen, and to me as the means of communication with her. I must get all her letters through him, for I could never make her simple heart and unbusiness-like head comprehend the necessity for my taking a false name in England. She would be frightened at the mere idea, and she must never know it. This necessity alone would oblige me to endeavour to establish thoroughly good relations between Helen and Trenton Warren before I sail to-morrow.'

'Before I sail to-morrow.' The words turned his mind into a new train of thought. Absorbed, he let his chin recline upon his breast, and did not notice Helen's entrance at the other end of the supper-room. She was clad in a loose dressing-gown and looked lovely, with her hair hanging around her shoulders.

When she had progressed halfway up the room, her eyes were attracted by something shining on the ground just in front of her. Stooping and picking the object up, she found it to be a portion of a sleeve-link, an engraved cameo in a gold setting; the gold work had been twisted and broken under the feet of the throng. All this Helen saw at a glance; but placing it in the pocket of her dressing-gown, she thought no more of it, and entered the library to join her husband.

CHAPTER III.

THE SHADOW OF PARTING.

So absorbed was Alston in his rumination, that it was not until he felt Helen's gentle touch upon his shoulder that he was aware of her presence.

'Has my melancholy been infectious?' said she, bending tenderly over him, and bringing her face close to his. 'Is it possible that what I said about your going could have turned your thoughts in the same direction?'

'Not at all,' said he, with a half smile; 'my thoughts were of quite another kind. I was thinking—'

'Hush!' she said, laying her little hand softly on his lips. 'Don't say you were thinking of business; that hated rival displaces me in your mind far too much as it is, but to give up to it such moments as these would be sacrilege. I will be your sole consideration now, until—until—'

'Until the end of my life,' said Alston, passing his arm tenderly round her; 'and your jealousy of my absence and all those connected with it is a mere pretence, a playful pastime, as you very well know.'

'Let us settle it so,' said Helen, 'and quit the subject. Meanwhile,' she said, taking from her pocket a morocco case, 'I have a present for you, Alston, and one,' placing it in his hand, 'which I think you will like.'

He opened it, and saw gleaming on the blue velvet a plain but costly gold hunting-watch.

'Thanks, dearest one,' he said, taking it in his hand and looking tenderly up at her. 'I shall like it, because, by its aid, I shall check off every hour that brings me nearer to my home and to you.'

'Why, Alston,' said Helen, laying her hand tenderly on his, 'do you know that is quite a poetical sentence? I fear your reputation as a practical man would be lost for ever if it were known in Wall-street that you had given utterance to such a remark. But,' she added, taking the watch from him, 'it will have, I trust, a still stronger value in your eyes.'

She touched a spring, and the back flying open revealed an admirably executed coloured photograph, a likeness of herself; underneath was engraved the date, 'February 20th, 1871.'

'O, how glorious!' said Alston Griswold, with surprise. 'It is a wonderful likeness,' said he, after a little pause, during which he had been looking fondly at the picture; 'somewhat too sad and serious, perhaps, for my Helen.'

'It reflects the shadow of parting which hung over your Helen at the time it was taken, as the engraved date underneath will never cease to remind you; you see it, Alston, the one dark day in our married life.'

'You shall regard it in a very different light, dear one,' said her husband; 'you shall learn to look upon it as the day on which your husband entered into an undertaking by which his fortune was perfected, and he was left freed from the cares of business to devote the remainder of his existence to his wife and his home.'

'God grant it!' said Helen fervently. 'Each time that you look upon that picture, Alston, think upon what you have said just now, and come what may, make up your mind not to leave me alone again.'

'You speak of being alone, dear, as though you were on a desolate island, instead of in New York, surrounded by troops of friends.'

'I am always alone when I am without you; and as to friends, I am not sanguine as to their taking much interest in our

affairs, or helping me to smooth any difficulties which may arise in my path.'

'There is one, at least, among them of
whom you must not speak so lightly,' said
Alston in a grave voice; 'one who has
already been tried and proved himself in
the highest degree trustworthy, and in
whom my confidence is such that I am
about to ask him for further proof of his
friendship.'

Helen's glance shifted instantly from
her husband's face and dropped upon the
ground. She knew instinctively to whom
he was alluding. Should she in that last
moment give utterance to her detestation
and distrust? Should she implore Alston
to authorise her to deny herself to Mr.
Warren, and entreat him to select some
other friend as his agent in the transaction
of any business which might be necessary
between them? She paused for an instant
in reflection. What reason could she give
for such a course of action? What real and

tangible ground of complaint had she against this man? None at all. A vague dislike, an undefined suspicion, were all she could bring forward; and these her husband's practical common sense would induce him, with all his love for her, to reject at once.

'I am glad that we possess such a friend, Alston,' said Helen, after a pause. 'I say "we," because, allied as we are, not merely formally but in heart, without the smallest shade of division between us, this mysterious unknown could not be your friend without, as it seems to me, being mine.'

'There is no mystery about me, dear one,' said Alston, 'for I am speaking of Trenton Warren; and as to his being your friend, he would only too gladly prove himself if you would give him greater opportunity of so doing.'

'Greater opportunity, Alston!' she cried. 'Have I then been remiss in—'

'Remiss in nothing which concerns the duties of a wife,' said he tenderly; 'only I thought I had noticed—it may have been imagination—that there was a certain coldness and avoidance in your manner towards Warren. He is himself somewhat of my temperament, Helen, engrossed in business, unaccustomed to make the polite advances common in society, and liable to take flight immediately if he did not find his attentions appreciated.'

The bitter word rose in Helen's mouth as she listened. 'I am sorry that Mr. Warren,' she commenced, and then better reflection came to her aid, and she broke off that sentence. 'I will not have you compare Mr. Warren to yourself,' she resumed, 'for there is no one like you in the world; but I have no doubt that Mr. Warren means very well, and I certainly had no intention of snubbing him, as you seem to fancy I have done.'

'That is spoken like my own true little wife,' said Alston. 'Then depend upon it,' he added, assuming an important air, which, under other circumstances, Helen would have found amusing, 'depend upon it that the knowledge of human nature which I possess would prevent my forming an intimate alliance with one who was not worthy of it, and I want you and Trenton Warren to be the best of friends. It will be the greatest comfort to me during my absence to know that I have left you in the charge of one who is worthy of the thorough confidence which we both equally place in him.'

'You—you are going to leave me in Mr. Warren's charge, Alston?'

'Why, Helen,' replied her husband, with a laugh, 'you speak as though you were a trembling captive and he a terrific gaoler into whose custody I was about to deliver you. When I say take charge, I mean simply this. During my absence it will be necessary that there should be some one to whom you can refer in any ordinary matters of your daily life, whom you can call into your council, and by whose decision you shall abide at any special crisis which that dear, unbusiness-like little brain might find itself unable to grapple with. For this confidential position there is no one so fitted as Trenton Warren. He knows both my private and my business affairs, has a cool clear head, and on more than one occasion has shown his devotion to my service. I have told him what is wanted of him, and he will accept the charge.'

Should she speak then? Should she seize what might be the last opportunity of declaring to him the dread, strong yet un-definable, which lay so heavy on her soul? Should she brave the chances of his rail-lery, his annoyance, even of his anger, by imploring him not to leave her in this man's power, not to give him any control whatso-ever over her actions, avowing at the same time frankly that, while she suspected Tren-ton Warren of deceit and double dealing, she could give no reason but that internal consciousness which, however powerful in its operations, had no practical value.

No, she would not do this; she would not send him forth on that desolate journey amongst strangers with any doubt or distrust at his heart. Better for her to bear whatever unpleasantness there might be in her relations with this man rather than perplex her husband during his absence with an additional source of anxiety. So she looked at him with a soft smile and said:

'It will doubtless be all right, Alston; and Mr. Warren and I shall get on very well together. I suppose I have formed an exaggerated idea of the horrors of this absence of yours. Mrs. Hotchkins, whose husband is so frequently called over to the other side, says that the time slips away without one's noticing it; and that she is quite surprised when she hears the vessel bringing him is telegraphed at Sandy Hook. I don't think surprise is exactly the phrase which will express my feelings when I get that welcome news.'

'No, my love; but, then, you are not

Mrs. Hotchkins. Nor have I, I hope, much in common with the eminent dry-goods man. But she is right, I daresay, as regards the quick passing of the time.'

'I suppose I shall hear from you constantly, Alston?'

'Certainly, dearest; by every mail.'

'And I suppose,' she said, glancing up at him with a demure look, 'that you will wish me to write to you occasionally?'

'Occasionally!' he cried. 'You must let me hear from you equally constantly. And, by the way, I have something to say to you about that—'

He checked himself just in time. He was on the point of explaining to her the arrangement he had made that all her letters to him should be sent under cover to Warren, but he thought it better to keep silence. Her simple nature never would understand the business necessity which induced him to adopt another name during his stay in England, in order that the nature and extent of his operations might not become known in Wall-street, and thus influence the position of certain transactions in which he was already known to be deeply engaged. Her trust in him, he flattered himself, was beyond question; but as he had never suffered her to have the slightest knowledge of business matters (with which indeed she had shown no inclination to meddle), she could not be supposed to comprehend that what he intended to do was what was constantly done for the purpose of preventing one's rivals from getting a trade advantage, but would look upon it as a deception which no honourable man ought, under any circumstances, to permit himself to practise.

Alston Griswold then made up his mind that he would not intrust his wife with this part of his intentions on the spot, but would send her word of it only by the letter of instructions which he had already written, and which, on the eve of his departure and well

on board the ship, he would give to Warren
to take to her.   Warren was aware of and
approved of his project of taking a false
name ; and Warren's judgment was, in
Alston's eyes, indisputable.   He would defer letting Helen know about it until he
was safely out of reach of objection.

'You said you had something to say to
me about that,' said Helen, recalling him to
the conversation; 'you seem to have fallen
into a reverie.'

'It was but a temporary one, dearest,
and is immediately dispelled by the sound
of your voice,' said Alston Griswold, rousing himself.   'We were talking about your
letters to me, and what I want to say to
you is this, that you must write every day.'

'Every day!' cried Helen, in astonish-
ment.   'There is not a mail every day,
Alston; you would receive several by the
same post, and find quite a jumble of news.'

'Nevertheless, you must write every
day,' he said with a smile, 'though what

you write need not be posted; and as to letters, I do not intend you to send me letters at all; I intend you to keep a diary.'

'A diary!' she echoed; 'I never did such a thing in my life. I have begun a dozen, kept them up bravely for the first day or two, forgotten them for a week, and then descended into a series of entries "nothing particular."'

Griswold laughed. 'That was because you had other things to engross your mind; now I hope your diary will be your one absorbing topic. It will be the sole record I shall ever see of your daily life, which, though absent, I hope and know I shall in a certain sense fill, and it therefore must be all-interesting and all-important to me.'

'You have thoroughly studied my weak points, Alston,' said Helen, with a smile, 'and know that that is an argument that I cannot withstand—the journal shall be kept.'

'Kept from day to day, copiously and

full of detail,' said her husband; 'do not omit anything because you may think it trivial or uninteresting; the trivialities are probably what will interest me most. Let me be able to follow your life from day to day through all the familiar hours of it, and thus endeavour to cheat myself out of the sense of separation.'

As he spoke these last words, he bent down, and encircling her with his arms, pressed her to his heart. 'Now let us go and see the child,' he said—'my little unconscious rival. If she had not existed, you would have accompanied me on this trip to the old country, and I consider myself exceedingly generous in still retaining my affection for her.'

The Cuba was advertised to sail at three P.M., but early the next morning the house in Fifth-avenue was astir, and with all the bustle and confusion occasioned by its master's impending departure. Huge boxes, packages of coats and rugs and piles of clothing, removed from drawers and submitted to inspection before being packed, lumbered up the passage; heterogeneous articles, from paper parcels up to portmanteaus, were continually arriving, their bearers bringing with them little notes, the writers of which expressed their hope that they were not giving their friend too much trouble in asking him 'just to take this across with him;' friends who lived in the neighbourhood, and did not care to take the trouble of going down to the ship, dropped in to say good-bye, and were found wandering all over the house in search of its owner.

And in the midst of all this confusion and all this crowd, Helen drifted purposelessly about, spoken to by everybody, but scarcely comprehending what was said to her, and when replies were desired, answered them vaguely, her eyes filled with tears, her heart sinking more and more

within her as she watched the hand creep
ing round the dial, and bringing nearer and
nearer the hour at which her husband was
to start.

It had been originally intended that she
should accompany Alston to the ship and
take leave of him on board, but she had
abandoned that idea.   It would have been
impossible for her, she felt, to have main-
tained her calmness at such a moment, and
for his sake, as well as for her own, she determined on not making the attempt.

And now the time had come!   She saw
it in his face as he slowly made his way up
the stairs to where she stood in the door-
way of her boudoir—her own room where
they had spent such happy times, and from
the wall of which his portrait was even
then looking at her with something of a sad
expression.

Alston took her by the hand and drew
her gently into the room, closing the door
behind him.

' The carriage is at the door, darling,' he said in broken tones, 'and I have not given myself much more than time to get across to the Cunard wharf. For both our sakes let us make this scene of parting as short as possible. My darling, my own heart's darling, God bless and protect you! Recollect the diary; let it be begun to-morrow and write it fully and freely. Once more, my own one, farewell !'

He held her yielding form to his heart, pressed one long, long kiss upon her lips, and was gone.

When the carriage drove into the yard of the Cunard wharf in Jersey City, Alston Griswold saw at a glance that half New York had come to see him off. He had caught sight of several friends on board the ferry-boat, but had no idea of their real number until they clustered round him as he alighted. Wall-street, of course, was well represented. There was Uncle Dick, rubicund and genial, smacking his lips as though the flavour of the terrapin which he had eaten for luncheon at the corner of Chambers-street still hung about his palate; and at his elbow, of course, was bright-eyed handsome Billy Barstow, with his hand on every one's shoulder, and his rich voice proclaiming every one to be his 'dear old boy,' ready, not merely by word, but in deed, to do universal kindness. And there was Alf Macgregor, the banker, whom no amount of American citizenship could deprive of his keen honest Scottish look and sharp incisive accent, and Willersheim and Schönbrunn, and all the Hebraic-German clique, and scores of others, to many of whom Alston Griswold had 'done a good turn,' and all of whom wished him well.

There was to be a final drink—a parting bumper of champagne—in the saloon, and, followed by the enthusiastic crowd, Alston made his way on board. But first he took a look at the chief-steward's cabin, which had been retained for his use, and which he found literally overflowing with baskets of flowers and floral offerings in pretty and quaint devices. Some of these were anonymous tributes, others bore the owners' cards; but there was one on which his eye at once rested—a large circular basket of primroses, with, in its centre, made of the freshest and choicest violets, 'Come back.' It did not give Alston Griswold much trouble to know who was the donor of that basket, or how fervent was the prayer expressed in that gift. This thought was put to flight by the arrival of Billy Barstow, who came to inform Alston that the champagne was ready in the saloon and that he alone was waited for.

'Give him two minutes with me first,' said Trenton Warren, suddenly looking over Barstow's shoulder. 'I want to speak to him on business, Billy, and I will then hand him over safely to you convivial boys.'

'I was looking anxiously for you, Tren-

ton,' said Griswold, when Barstow had retired; 'I want, as you know, to make you
the recipient of my last words. Here,' taking it from his pocket and handing it to his
friend, 'is the final letter of instructions for
Helen, telling her, among other matters,
that her letters are to come to me under
cover from you. I count upon you to place
this in her hands yourself.'

'You may rely upon my doing so,' said
Warren.

'And at once, if you please,' said Griswold.

'By at once you mean to-day,' said Warren. 'Have you told Mrs. Griswold to expect a visit from me?'

'No, I have not; but that need make
no difference, you know.'

'Of course not,' said Warren. 'Anything more?'

'Yes,' said Griswold, taking a slip of
paper from his pocket, 'the name under
which I propose to pass in England.'

Warren took the paper and glanced at it.

'All right,' he said, with a smile, 'that will do very well; not remarkable and yet not suspiciously common for a man doing big business—we consider it adopted. Now we must hurry to the saloon, the time is just up.'

The saloon was reached, the God-speed toast was drunk with all the honours, Warren and the New Yorkers returned to the shore, and the big ship noiselessly and almost invisibly headed into the stream and stood away upon her ocean voyage cheerily, cheerily.

'He had not warned her that I should come to-day,' said Trenton Warren to himself, as he landed from the ferry at Desbrosses-street, 'so that I shall not attempt to intrude upon her grief. The delivery of the letter will do very well to-morrow, and will give me a night during which to deliberate on my plan of action.'

The next day about noon Trenton Warren called at the house in Fifth-avenue, and was told by the servant that Mrs. Griswold was not well enough to receive visitors.

'Take her this card, if you please,' he said quietly, 'and tell her that I am the bearer of a message from Mr. Griswold.'

In a few minutes the servant returned.

'Walk this way, if you please,' she said; 'Mrs. Griswold will see you.' And muttering to himself, 'I thought so,' Trenton Warren marched onward to the assault.

CHAPTER IV.

'I AM to write my letters to him, Alston says, in the form of a journal, so that when I send them off each week, he may be able " to follow my life from day to day through all the familiar hours of it, and so to cheat himself out of the sense of separation." These are Alston's words, not mine; I have it not in me to think these thoughts, and so the words would not come.

'And why, I wonder? Am I a heartless woman, or ungrateful, or only commonplace, and unable to understand the way in which things present themselves to Alston? At all events, it will do me no good to think about myself; I shall come to no better liking for myself, to no clearer conclusion about myself, by questions of this kind. If

I cannot quite understand him, I can at least perfectly obey him, and, please God, I will do that, as I have always done it; and as he has said I am to keep a journal, I will keep a journal. So I begin it thus, in an irregular and unskilful fashion, no doubt, but with the utmost sincerity of intention to write in it everything which can interest him (according to his scale and meaning of interest, not of my own), on the very day after his departure.

'As I know that nothing can be regularly done which is not done at a set hour, I will begin my journal with a rule for the writing of it. It is to be for Alston; it is to be his share in the day during his absence, and it shall be done during that hour when I was always with him, just before I went up-stairs to see baby fast asleep, and to go to bed myself; after every one was gone, when we had company at home; when we had returned, if we had been out, and when we compared notes of our impressions of the place and the people. In Alston's room, at Alston's desk, my letter-journal shall be written, and it may be I shall get over the shyness and the discomfort with which the notion of writing to him inspires me now, in the custom and familiarity of the time, and be able to persuade myself that I am only talking to him.

'This, of course, is not beginning; this is only a little rehearsal, what the jockeys call "a preliminary canter;" I shall start properly by and by. It is rather odd, when I come to think of it, that I have never written to Alston in my life, beyond one or two mere notes just before we married; and he found fault with them, and said they were stiff and formal, and such as I might have written to my writing-master, to show him how I had profited by his instructions, and how attentively I looked to my downstrokes and my loops. I remember thinking that though Alston said this in jest he was very nearly right, for I had made three or four fair copies of each note before I sent it, which was only my foolish girl's notion of respect for Alston after all, for I am sure I never copied out anything I ever wrote to Thornton in my life, but just sent it as it was, dashed off anyhow. This makes it all the more difficult to write to Alston now, and in journal form too; it is commencing a new correspondence and learning a new art.

'I have never written down any of the things that have happened to me ; I have just let them slip by as if they were things in a picture or in a dream, and I am a good way on in my life now—a wife and a mother, to say nothing at all of my girlhood and the story that was in it, only a simple story, but the kind of thing women, I should think, remember always, and I suppose and hope it will be a simple story now until the end, until Alston and I shall bid baby good-bye in this world.

'And I hope that day will come for me

before it comes for Alston, for I cannot imagine what I should do with or for baby without him. He says I am not a helpless but a useful woman, and could stand alone as well as the avowedly "strong" ones if I had to do it; but, I don't know, I think Alston is wrong; I fancy the only bit of strength I have about me is the power of hiding my weakness—well, there's some defence in that, after all. But O, the pain of knowing oneself to be a coward! the pain of feeling as I feel this horrid presentiment of evil in Alston's journey to England, of not being able to hide it *quite*, and to make the going, which he feels so much, a little easier to him!

'But this talking to myself is not beginning my journal. It is really very difficult to write the everyday history of one's life in a disjointed unpremeditated way. Here have I been sitting for the last twenty minutes staring at the paper, and not writing a line. I cannot bring myself before myself, as it were—something to be described and set down in black and white.

'What have I to tell Alston, except that I am writing in my room quite early in the morning—not as I intend to write in future, when all the house is quiet, and baby is still fast asleep? I could not sleep last night for loneliness and trouble, and this haunting something, which is not presentiment, I suppose, but merely nervousness, and which I must put down with resolution if I am to be cheerful and useful. This order of Dr. Benedict, that I am to give up nursing baby, is troubling me. I feel that he is right; I am not equal to it, and I should harm the child and myself; and yet I hate the very idea of putting a strange woman in my own place—a strange woman, just picked up by an advertisement! If this is to be my journal, it will be nothing but a list of grievances. Sometimes, ungrateful woman that I am, I think life is not much more.

'A happy idea has just occurred to me. Suppose I write my journal in a retrospective sense? Suppose I bring myself before myself as I was, and thus make it easier to take up the history of myself as I am? All the earlier portion will be for myself, and when I come abreast of the present time, I will write it for Alston.

'The notion pleases me; I had almost forgotten myself as I was, and now I shall live within my own sight over again. I have bought such a pretty book, in vellum binding, with gilded leaves and lock, and in that I am going to write the story of my childhood and my girlhood, for no eyes but my own—and Thornton's when I am dead, if he lives longer than I do, as Heaven grant he may—he, too, as well as Alston. I will shut myself up; I will see no one. I will work hard, and by this day week I shall have written up to the present and done my letter so as to mail it to Europe.'

Into her pretty book, in vellum binding, with gilded leaves and lock, Mrs. Alston Griswold pasted the foregoing prefatory pages; and then settled herself seriously to her task, and wrote as follows:

'My life commenced with the greatest misfortune which can signalise the beginning of any existence: My mother died shortly after my birth. How much more I should have had to remember, how many more pleasures, how much happiness, if I had ever been to any one what baby is to me! Every one was very kind to me, and I was a happy child; but there was nothing very particular in my childhood except about my going to school, and that is particular, because it brought Thornton and me together and did away with my loneliness. For I certainly was lonely when father was away at the Mills all day, and aunt Catherine busy all day long about the house, evidently finding me very much in the way, and so glad when papa sent me to bed early, and she could have those long talks with him, which, I felt certain, made papa so depressed and melancholy next day.

'If I were writing a novel now, and had to draw a picture of home—Holland Mills was its commonplace name—I wonder could I make it all picturesque and interesting? I don't think I could; and yet the long low green and white house was pretty—and the fields, the orchards, the river, were all beautiful to me. I could describe every part of the road between the Mills and the minister's house, Thornton's home—for Thornton's father was our minister, and his mother was our school-madam; but the minister did the most of the teaching.

'My place was beside Thornton on the very first day when aunt Catherine took me to school, and he became my friend and protector, and I his plague and oppressor, from that instant. What patience he had with me! and how naughty I was! I was a pretty child, and always very trim and neat : aunt Catherine never would have tolerated any untidiness or disorderly ways, and I regarded Thornton's plain features, much too large for his narrow face, and his untidy clothes, worn anyhow and much patched and darned, with great contempt. But Thornton soon made me ashamed of such a feeling. He helped me with my tasks, he even did some of them for me; he taught me to feel a moderate degree of interest in the subjects of our studies, in which he repeatedly shot far beyond me; he got me out of scrapes, and kept me out of mischief; he defended me against my adversaries, fought and punished them; he saved the life of my little dog, when it was drowning in the millstream, at the risk of his own (poor little Taffy! she is stuffed and under a glass case in Alston's study; and that is more of Alston's kindness to me, for I am sure he does not like her, and she *isn't* naturally done); he stole apples for me, and he lent me his own skates in the ice-season, when aunt Catherine would not hear of my having a pair.

'I put these foolish-sounding trifling things down because I want to bring back to myself the assurance that Thornton was always like a brother to me.

'The first thing that I can remember as troubling the busy tranquillity of my school life was my coming to understand why aunt Catherine and papa always had so much to talk about, and why the talking never did them any good. I was growing up into a staid little person, as Alston says I am now, when the word "difficulties" began to be familiar to me. It never has the sad and hopeless meaning in America that it has in the old countries of Europe, I am told; but "difficulties" are not easy or pleasant anywhere, and papa was not a man to bear them well. He gave way very much, and I used to tell Thornton about it, and he and I used to consult together and discuss what could be done.

'Thorton had only one solution to offer; it was that he should marry me. This, he said, would save a great deal of expense, by taking me completely off my father's hands. But I saw that that plan would not be of much use, because some one must have given us something to live upon, and that some one would certainly not have been Thornton's father; for he was very poor, and Thornton was studying as hard as he could, that he might be able to go into business and assist his father. So that idea did not come to anything; and when we were a year older, and the "difficulties" were a year worse, Thornton got a situation in New York, and he and I parted.

'It was very hard—very hard indeed— to part: I don't mean to deny that or to make any mistake with myself about it; but I do wish to assert most distinctly, though only for my own satisfaction, that there never was any engagement between Thornton and me.

'I know Thornton loved me as a man loves a woman whom he would make the partner of his life—as Alston loves me, but without Alston's curious notion of the essential difference and distance between men and women. Thornton, though a highly-cultivated man, thought me perfectly capable of understanding the best of his studies, if not of following their details, of sharing his interest in every sense; but Alston could not think thus, and though he is most tender and indulgent, he is not confidential. I should be the most ungrateful of women were I to murmur; but I do wish sometimes for a little more confidence, even at the cost of a little less indulgence.

'But I am wandering from my intention to record exactly what was the state of things between Thornton and me when our schooldays came to an end, and he went to take a small post with but poor pay at New

York. I know that he loved me—that was frankly acknowledged between us; but there was no thought that we should marry, then or ever. I loved him too; but not with love such as I have heard and read of, but have never known; love which must mean misery, I think, because it causes one to sacrifice duty, and common sense, and all one's obligations towards other people, to its own imperious claims. I knew that I could not be Thornton's wife without harming him and all concerned; and that, however much I might believe that it would be the happiest fate to be his wife, happiness of that particular kind was not destined to be mine. I do not say our parting was not sad, but I am quite safe in saying that it was not bitter.

‘A little while after Thornton went away to New York I first saw Alston. He came to Holland Mills on some business connected with papa's affairs, and merely in a business capacity. My father and he had not met previously, and we knew nothing of him except that he was a prosperous merchant of New York, and I think we had a little of the sense of shrinking and depression—I mean aunt Catherine and I had—which comes to unprosperous people in the sight of those whose lot is far different. A very little time, a very brief acquaintance with Mr. Griswold, did away with such a feeling as this, and turned him into a friend.

'My father took to him from the first, and as to aunt Catherine, I never knew her to like any man who was not a minister so much, or to believe in him so implicitly. He brought relief and cheerfulness with him, that was plain, and at first all he did was quite for papa's sake. After a while, he began to care very much about me, and, like a gentleman, as he is in everything, he told me that he loved me, and hoped I might in time come to love him well enough to marry him, but that I must not regard the matter as having anything whatever to do with the efforts he was making on my father's behalf. He would continue them as zealously as ever, whether I decided for or against him.

'I can never forget how Alston appeared that day. I had not thought about loving him, though of course I knew, as every woman knows such things, how he felt towards me; but when he spoke this to me, I felt that it would not be hard to love such a man, and that it would be a blessed fate to become his wife.

'He did not press me for an answer then; he said I must consider it until his next visit, and I promised him that I would do so. But before his next visit, ah, what a change had fallen on us all! My father had met with a terrible accident in the mill; he was hopelessly injured, and when Alston came it was to see him on his death-bed.

'The last hours of my dear father would have been very sad had it not been for

Alston. All was confusion in his affairs; there had not been time to disentangle them, as Alston was striving to do, and he could not have died in peace without the assurance which Alston gave him that aunt Catherine and I should be well cared for. He would not tell my father that he had asked me to marry him, because he feared my father might ask me for a promise made to *himself,* and so fetter the freedom of my will; but when I understood this reticence and the high honour that dictated it, and how much it would rejoice my father and take the sting from his death to know that I should be safe, with *such* safety, I told him in Alston's presence that he had asked me to be his wife, and that I had reserved the answer until now. My father placed my hand in Alston's, and from that moment I believe not one care belonging to this world troubled him. He told aunt Catherine that he did not wish any needless delay to be made about the marriage, that it should take place when a decent time should have elapsed after his death.

'When the sad funeral was over, as soon as I could bear to see him, I told Alston all about Thornton. The "all" was not very much, but he still more fully proved to me that he was a high-minded man by the way in which he heard it, and the un-asked promise which he gave me that Thornton's interests should also be his care. He could not do anything to help him just then, without sending to New York for him (I have omitted to mention that Thornton had got a better berth than his first, and gone to New Orleans), but there was something which he had in view that he thought would exactly suit him likely to turn up after a while.

'He wished me to write at once to Thornton and tell him of my approaching marriage, but not to mention his intention of serving him; that, he said, would come more graciously afterwards. I did write to

Thornton, but he did not answer my letter until he addressed me as Alston's wife, and then I did not hear from him again for a long time—he had gone on a trip to the Dominion for his employers—not until just before baby was born.

'But I am not jotting down my own story, for, after all, there is not much of Thornton in that, though I seem to put a great deal of him in this. Our wedding was a very quiet one, and on my wedding-day I took leave of the Mills.

'Alston wound up all poor papa's affairs, sold the place, paid the debts, and arranged for aunt Catherine's boarding at Mrs. Broom's very near our house in New York. Alston proposed, in his delicate generous way, to make aunt Catherine's allowance appear to come from the sale, that she should still suppose herself to be under obligation to her brother only; but I soon made him understand that would be a hopeless attempt. There is not a better head for business in the States than aunt Catherine's, and she understood papa's affairs as well as he did; she could not have been misled about the origin of a dollar.

'But, as I told Alston, she and I are not of the mean sort who hate to be obliged to a friend because we feel ourselves incapable of gratitude; we both accepted his kindness as loyally as he offered it, and I don't think there is a happier old lady in New York than aunt Catherine—with baby, who has cut me out completely, to come and see, and unlimited sermons to listen to—Mrs. Broom's boarding-house goes in for ministers, and they have several denominations there.

'I was bewildered when Alston brought me home. It took me some little time to get accustomed to the luxurious house, and the stir of society, and even to the fact of living in a city. I felt too small, too young, and too ignorant. But Alston helped me, Alston encouraged me, Alston had perfect patience with me; and if he would only have made me more of a confidant, and less of an idol, I should have had not one unfulfilled wish.

'All this shall be for his return, please God. I am growing older so rapidly, so much older than is told by years, and when he sees me a sensible mother, he cannot help thinking I am fit to be regarded as a wise wife.

'But I must stop. It is baby's bed-time, and I can go on when she and I are dressed, until lunch. This really must be put in journal form, "posted up" to yesterday, before to-night, that I may keep my promise to Alston—the promise he asked me with almost his last kiss—"You will be sure to begin to-morrow."'

CHAPTER V.

AN EXPLANATION.

HELEN GRISWOLD laid down her pen; placed the sheet of paper which she had just covered with her neat writing in a drawer of her davenport; ranged her natty desk implements, and then, resting her chin in the palms of her hands and looking wistfully before her, she fell a-thinking. Was the sense of her husband's absence growing real and painful? Had the effort of this unwonted method of communication with him roused her to a realisation of the great change that had fallen upon her daily life? Perhaps so. But there was more perplexity than pain in Helen's face, and Griswold's departure, though painful, was in no way perplexing. There was something lurking in her mind to-day—there had been something lurking in her mind yesterday—which she dreaded to call out and gaze upon in the open light.

After a little she rose restlessly, and with an impatient sigh, and passed into the adjoining room, where she found her infant just awake, and was soon absorbed in the pleasant duties and interest of her nursery. Then came a walk with the child and its nurse, and Helen reëntered her house, feeling composed and cheerful, and full of good resolutions for the wise disposition of her time during her husband's absence; a disposition by which she almost unconsciously provided for the elimination of the one disturbing depressing element.

She had just reached her room and was laying aside her bonnet when the servant brought a message from Mr. Warren. That gentleman requested that he might be admitted to her presence, and said that he had come upon special business from Mr. Griswold.

'He knows how to make me receive him,' Helen thought bitterly; and her eyes flashed and her brows contracted. 'He knows I cannot let the maid take a refusal to such a plea as that.'

'Tell Mr. Warren I will be with him in a few minutes,' she said; and went on mechanically arranging her dress.

As she was fastening her linen cuffs, she was reminded of the trifling incident of the finding of the sleeve-link, and it occurred to her that the ornament in question belonged to Trenton Warren. Surely it was a carved gem; one of a pair which she had seen him wear, respectively representing the heads of Hebe and Ganymede. She was glad to have recollected this circumstance; it would give her something indifferent, something safe, to talk about. She looked about for the link; she had taken it out of her pocket the night before, and laid it down on her dressing-table. It was not there. She called her maid, and asked her if she had noticed a gentleman's sleeve-link in the ring-tray. Her maid replied that she had seen it, and supposing it to belong to Mr. Griswold, she had slipped it into his dressing-bag just before he closed it. Mrs. Griswold remarked carelessly that it was rather provoking, that the sleeve-link was not Mr. Griswold's, but that it could not be helped, and it did not matter.

She lingered, unwilling to go down, and hoping, when at length she could not defer doing so any longer, that as soon as Mr. Warren should have informed her of the nature of the business, real or pretended, on which he had come, some other visitor might arrive and interrupt the *tête-à-tête*, which was extremely disagreeable to her in prospect and most ill-timed.

It was impossible longer to loiter, and Mrs. Griswold went down-stairs, her long dress trailing, her small head rather disdainfully held up and back, her countenance wearing an expression which all her cus-

tomary associates, save one, would have
regarded with surprise. In the presence of
that one, whose ear had caught her first
footfall upon the thickly-carpeted stairs, she
stood in a few moments, and his glance
caught the unfamiliar expression and read
it aright—without, indeed, its inmost meaning, its complications of origin, but still
clearly enough.

Trenton Warren was standing in the
same place from whence he had watched
her so closely on the night which had so
severely taxed his self-command and her
patience.

He was handsomely dressed in his usual
accurate unexaggerated style, in a light
gray morning suit, and he had an air of
perfect leisure about him, simple leisure
which was not without its charm.

It was the kind of manner which pleases
women who live in a business atmosphere,
among men who are generally either occupied or over-tired ; it said so intelligibly,

'Here I am entirely devoted to your service, having got everything off my mind but yourself.'

As all the women of his acquaintance knew Trenton Warren to be as busy a man as his fellows, the compliment was real, and so the manner was effective. He was decidedly liked by women; perhaps the solitary exception to that rule was the one woman for whom he wore this manner most elaborately, most watchfully, most invariably. But Helen Griswold did not like even the air of leisure which was so captivating to other women. It had the misfortune to link itself to the one drawback, the one discomfort, the one injury of her life, and so, woman-like, she distorted its meaning, she refused its tribute.

He, too, she bitterly thought, had the presumption to regard her as an ornament, as a being incompetent to fill a serious and sympathetic place in her husband's life; he, too, held that women should be excused

from business, and so he came to her a
totally unreal creature, a drawing-room
lounger, with malice in his quiet smile and
insulting depreciation under his deferential
address, and the acquiescence in her useless-
ness which encouraged Alston in his one
fault, and made her heart sick with a powerless anger, to which her unerring woman's
instinct, as she called it—the least trustworthy guide any woman can follow except
within a very limited track—assured her
that Trenton Warren was perfectly conscious.

He had never found her in a less conciliatory humour than on the present occasion. The undefined struggle in her own
heart, the signs that a great change was
passing over her, the introspection which
had been so entirely foreign to her mind
and habits, the little lingering bitterness
which had mingled with the solemn tenderness of a parting with Alston, imparted
into it by her feeling that she in reality

knew nothing about the purpose and details of the business which was taking him so far away from her for so long; all this had prepared her to receive his visit with anything but welcome. And as he looked at her he knew that, too, and she saw that he knew it.

Helen Griswold was not sufficiently a woman of the world to be mistress of those fine shades of manners which are such powerful weapons on the woman's side of social warfare; but she conveyed to Trenton Warren with quite sufficient accuracy a sense that she expected him to deliver his message and go, before they had exchanged two sentences. She did not take her customary seat, but placed herself on an ordinary chair in an attitude which had a provoking coolness about it; and she looked over, not at Trenton.

He had seen her husband later than she had; her husband's parting words had been for him; would she not display some curiosity as to the final interview—some interest? Not she; not a jot! So he made up his mind at once that he would not use any *ménagements* with her, but show her at once and plainly the position in which 'that enviable ass, Griswold'—for thus Mr. Trenton Warren called his confiding absent friend in his thoughts—had placed her.

'You have some business to be communicated to my husband, I believe?' said poor Helen, with her very best imitation of slightly patronising unconcern.

'O dear, no,' replied Warren, putting his hand into his breast-pocket and taking out a letter. 'I have no business to communicate *to* Mr. Griswold; my commission is *from* him.'

'To me?' The colour flushed over her face.

'To you,' he answered with a bow, and then went on without looking at her, his eyes bent on the letter in his hand. 'You are aware that I met Mr. Griswold at the steamer. He had some last words to say to me—last words which gratified me very much, Mrs. Griswold, because they proved the sincerity and genuineness of his confidence in me; he intrusted me with—'

'That letter, which I can see from here is addressed to me. Please to give it to me, sir!'

He glanced at her very slightly, smiled also very slightly, and laid the letter on the table, by her side. She had not made the least gesture like taking it from his hand.

'I thank you,' she said, but did not take up the letter. 'I thought my husband had given me his final instructions; but perhaps he had forgotten something. I am sorry you should have had the trouble of coming during business hours.' Then with a total change of tone, 'I think you lost a sleeve-link here the other evening, which I picked up; but most unfortunately it has—'

'Excuse me, Mrs. Griswold,' said Warren, in a firm tone, 'if in my turn I inter-

rupt you.   I have something to say, and I
do not wish to turn to irrelevant matters
until it has been said.   I did not come
here merely to bring you a letter, which I
might have sent you by a messenger; I
came here for a more serious purpose,
which may or may not be corroborated by
Mr. Griswold's letter—I know nothing of
its contents—to tell you that your husband
has intrusted you to my care, and wished
you to refer to me in his absence in any
case in which you might experience difficulty or require advice.'

So far Helen had heard him with varying
colour and a beating heart, half choked with
anger and an undefined dread; but now she
rose, and laying her hand upon the letter,
said, in an unsteady voice, ' Your communication is an extraordinary one, Mr. Warren.   I think—I think you can hardly expect me to say that it is welcome.   I would
rather read my husband's letter before I
hear more.'

'You wish me to leave you?' asked Warren, who had risen when she rose, but made no sign of an intention to go away.

'I do.'

'I cannot obey you, Mrs. Griswold. Let me beg that you will resume your seat and listen to me. I am an unwelcome visitor, I know, and you take my communication badly for some reason which I do not understand, but which I hope to surmount.'

He controlled himself perfectly; his tone was quite deferential, and not the faintest, most flickering smile passed over his face.

She had slowly reseated herself, and sat holding the letter and looking at him with a fixed frown.

'Griswold felt this parting, in more than its sentimental aspect, very seriously—he thought of your position gravely, and of your inexperience and habitual dependence upon him for guidance. He deputed me, as his most intimate friend—indeed, the

only one who is thoroughly acquainted with
the business which has taken him to England—to act for him in several affairs here
—things with which I need not trouble you
—and to take care of you and baby; I
use his own words. · In the first place, I
must apprise you that all your letters to
your husband—the charming daily record
which you have promised him' (Helen
started and winced with pain. That her
husband should have talked so familiarly of
her with any man—with this man of all
men!)—'must reach him through me.'

'Through you? I do not understand
what you mean.'

'Then I will make my meaning plainer.
Every letter which you write to your husband must be sent to my office, under cover
to me, to be forwarded from thence. Such
are Griswold's explicit directions. Please
to look at this memorandum.'

He laid a leaf, torn from a note-book,
before her; it bore these words:

'*All letters written to me by my wife, or sent to my private address to be forwarded, are to be sent under cover to Trenton Warren to his office, when he will dispatch them to me.*

'ALSTON GRISWOLD.'

'I see,' said Helen, 'that your statement is correct, that Mr. Griswold has made this extraordinary arrangement, and that, much as I dislike it, I am bound to conform to it. But you, Mr. Warren, *you* are bound to explain it. Have the goodness to do so.'

'Ah, ha!' he replied, with a shrug of the shoulders, full of impertinent depreciation to her angered eyes; 'that, I regret to say, it is not in my power to do!'

'What, do you pretend that after your last words with my husband, after undertaking the charge he laid upon you, after bringing me this letter and this memorandum, you do not know *why* Mr. Griswold made such an arrangement?'

'Pardon me, I do not pretend, I do not

say, anything of the sort. I am perfectly well aware of the motive which led to Mr. Griswold's making the arrangement which is unpleasant to you, but which I am constrained to commend as a wise and proper one. I merely say that I regret that it is not in my power to inform you of his reasons.'

'You refuse to tell me; you acknowledge that you are in my husband's confidence more completely than I am—you tell me so in fact, commending his unexplained directions to me—and you expect me to tolerate all this. For what do you take me, Mr. Warren?'

The struggle in Helen's mind and feelings while she spoke these brave-sounding words was severe. Under the smooth leisurely manner of Warren there was an ill-disguised consciousness of power which frightened her, and there was that nameless something that had already been haunting her. She was not exactly a courageous, but

she was a singularly sincere woman, and
there is always more or less bravery in
truthful actions. She made a sudden resolution even while her blood was cold, as she
asked the question of herself: ' Has Alston
put himself in this man's power ?' · She
would quarrel with Warren *à l'outrance* then
and there. She would put an end to this
evil influence in her life; it should haunt
her no longer. She would justify herself to
Alston if he blamed her by confiding in him,
as she had not yet done by telling him, the
inmost dread of her heart. If he treated it
as a folly, she would say let it be a folly in
his eyes, *let it be a folly of hers*, which she
should look to him to respect. A full presentiment and an intimation which she truly
and fully believed (there was a dash of
superstition about Helen Griswold)—with
which women with more mind than any
one who has taken the trouble to develop,
and an unconsciously unsatisfied heart one
occasionally possessed—told her that in an

utter breach with this man, a determined
stand against him, lay her only safety. She
would make the utter breach now on the
spot; she would take a determined stand.

With the wonderful quickness of thought,
all this passed through her mind, and her
resolution was taken before Trenton Warren answered her angry question, which he
did with considerable deliberation. He,
too, had been making a resolution; he, too,
recognised this interview as a crisis in his
relations with this woman—this woman so
beautiful in his sight, so captivating, so far
removed—unless, indeed, his skill and dar-
ing, his 'good play,' as he called it in his
inmost thoughts, chanced to bring her near.
The events of that morning had curtailed
the space between them in an unexpected,
unlooked-for manner. And he entirely misinterpreted the irrepressible symptoms of
emotion in Helen's manner. He saw that,
with all her braving out of the position, she
was afraid of him; and, as he judged her

only from the shallow depths of his own consciousness, as one who did not love her husband with passion, and therefore did not love
him at all, it never occurred to him that she
feared him for her husband's sake—he
sought and found a meaner motive for her
fear. Why should she fear him? Why
should she shrink from the notion of his influence with the husband she assuredly did
not love, if she were unconscious that he
had not an influence over herself which she
dreaded? Fear comes not of indifference,
nor is one with disdain! The hope which
he had secretly cherished in his treacherous
breast in a smouldering state for months
past sprang up into a flame under the influence of Helen's misinterpreted anger. The
mental process in his case was as swift as in
hers, and it was after only a brief pause between question and answer that he replied
to her.

'I refuse to tell you, Mrs. Griswold. It
is impossible that I should violate your hus-

band's injunctions on this point, and I hasten to reply to your other question. I do
expect you to tolerate my conduct, because
you *must* recognise that honour dictates it,
though you may not understand what it
costs me; and I take you for the best of
wives and the most fascinating of women.'

He approached her as he spoke with his
hand held out, and a smile upon his face
which drove the last faint scruples of prudence far from the exasperated woman whom
he had so thoroughly roused; but Helen
rolled her chair some feet back upon the
castors, and, with a slight wave of her hand,
rejected his. Very beautiful she looked—
more beautiful than he had ever seen her—
her great eyes ablaze, so that they shone
like jewels, as she said:

'And *I* take *you* for the falsest of men.
You have always been my enemy, and I
have always known it—known it so long
and so well, felt it so constantly, that it is a
relief to me to tell you so. Keep this secret

from me! Do you think Alston will keep it, when I ask him to explain it to me? No; you know he will not, though you would have made me despise and distrust him, if you could. Yes, you would, and you tried, tried hard, for some purpose of your own—I do not know and I do not care for what purpose — to divide us utterly. You succeeded in part—thank God, only in part did you succeed! Alston would have made me his friend and confidant only for you. But you made him contemptuous of my intelligence; you persuaded him that women are unsafe in matters of business; you divided me from one-half my husband's life, and made it a mystery to me. But for you I should have been his companion in everything. I tell you, Mr. Warren, I distrusted you from the first. I saw you had an influence which you were using ill, I—'

'You did me the honour and yourself the injury of being jealous of me, Mrs. Griswold. It is a mistake which young wives

are apt to make with respect to their husbands' friends, and one which frequently
costs them a good deal.'

'I was not jealous of you,' she said in-
dignantly. 'I could not entertain so base
a feeling. Why should not Alston have
friends, as many and as close as he
pleased? But you were his enemy—not his
friend; because you were my enemy; because you would have degraded me if you
could—yes, degraded me, I repeat—by
making my husband treat me as a toy or
an indulged pet, not as an equal associate.'

'You are simply doing him a monstrous
injustice,' said Warren, with a sudden
abatement of sarcasm in his tone and manner, and a not unsuccessful assumption of
hurt-feeling, of deferential explanatoriness;
'you are imputing that which is in the
nature of the man to an external influence.
Griswold is a very good fellow, and my
best friend; but his notions of women, all
his theories about them, differ from mine

widely. He believes in the intellectual inferiority of women as he believes in their physical beauty, and likes it as much. Long before he married you, he told me a clever woman was, to his mind, an anomaly, and a clever wife a nuisance; that he did not believe any woman in the world could understand business or hold her tongue; and he meant to conduct his domestic relations, if he ever found any, on Hotspur's theory, and, while giving his wife all due credit for discretion, making sure that she "would not tell that which she did not know." This root of bitterness was none of my planting, nor have I watered it. You have spoken with harsh frankness to me, Mrs. Griswold; let me speak with frankness that shall not be harsh to you. I have contemplated your domestic life with pain—'

'Indeed, and why? It is an unenviable one.'

'So you believe, because you have little

experience and an unawakened heart. If you only knew what home might be, and love, the love of a man to whom you would be more than the fairest of women, the dearest of friends, the most trusted of counsellors, the sharer of every feeling, the companion of every thought! Would not that be the ideal of earthly happiness?'

His voice had become low, tender, and persuasive, and his words had a strange influence on Helen. She seemed to forget *him*, to be conscious of them only, to have been sent by them into a dream.

'Happiness more than earthly,' she said, as if to herself, hardly knowing that she spoke.

'Such happiness might have been yours. Be honest, be patient, be true with yourself and with me, and you must acknowledge that it could never have come with your marriage with Griswold. He is the best of fellows, but it is not in him to appreciate you. You are a woman for a man to love with his whole mind and with all the strength of his pride. If fate had made you *my* wife you would have been so loved.'

He moved a step nearer to her, and stepped before her, looking at her with eyes whose gaze she dared not meet.

'You may as well hear me out,' he went on, with a tremor in his voice; 'since your ill-placed suspicions have forced me to clear myself from the charge which you have brought against me, it is fair that you should listen to me. When you believed that I was estranging Griswold from you, undervaluing you to him, I was tortured with envy of his lot, and silent about you because I dared not speak to my friend of his wife lest he should—slow as his mind is, except when business is concerned—suspect that I loved her.'

'You are a wicked man,' cried Helen, rising from her chair and speaking almost inarticulately in a passion of rage, shame, and fear. The undefined thing which had been haunting her, the shadow with which she had refused to parley, the shapeless dread which had troubled the last hours of her husband's presence in his home, the phantom that had stolen to her side when she was recording the blameless thoughts of her innocent heart, had assumed form, consistency, and spoke to her with a human voice and undissembled speech. This, then, was what it had all meant, and the thing which she had feared had come upon her in a shape worse than her fears. It was this man's prejudice, continued dislike, that she had fancied were in the atmosphere of her home, tainting it, and filtering drops of poison into her cup of life; but now she found it was his love, his deadly, hateful, treacherous, dastardly love. Good God! How she loathed and feared him, for her husband had gone away and left her in this man's power. Without his aid she could not even communicate with him, and he—and he, he was free to write whatsoever he pleased to Alston. It said much for Helen's courage and principle that she never dreamt, in the moment when all this was fresh and clear and terrible before her, of any compromise. She would keep this man at defiance, she would brave him.

'You are a wicked man,' she said, 'a traitor to your friend, and a coward to me; you take a dastardly advantage of my unprotected position, and the blind confidence which my husband places in you, and you insult me in my solitude. Leave my house, sir, and send me at once my husband's address in England. I refuse to transmit my letters through you. I repudiate all acquaintance with you henceforth from this hour; and if you attempt to presume upon the mistake Alston has made, I shall inform him word for word of what has occurred today. Let me pass, sir, or I will ring for my servants!'

Warren had interrupted her on her way to the door, and was standing before it, his hand behind his back pressed upon the upper panel.

'She did not say she would tell him *whether or no*,' was his rapid reflection, and there was a gush of guilty hope in the thought, for this man believed women to be virtuous only in the degree in which also they were fools, and he held Helen to be no fool.

'I entreat you to pause,' he said gently, 'before you make a scandal in the house. I am resolved to speak to you, and nothing short of your making such a scandal can deter me. I have offended you by telling you the truth, only a little more deeply than you were previously offended. I am very unfortunate, but I have justified myself, and I repeat it; I love you—I love you as I have never even persuaded myself that I loved any other woman! I ask nothing—I seek nothing from you but the toleration of a sentiment which does you no dishonour, which is stronger than my will, for your husband's sake and your own.'

'And I tell you,' she cried, wild and reckless with anger, 'that I will not tolerate it, either for my husband's sake or my own, for it *does* me dishonour. It may be, as you say, that mine is an unawakened heart, but my conscience is unused to slumber' (in after days she remembered this fatal admission, and raged blindly and in vain against the impulse which had induced her to make it), 'and now I am not going to make any scandal, I am not going to endeavour to pass that door until you think fit to stand aside and no longer use virtual violence to me in my own house. See, I resume my seat; I shall retain it until you rid me of your presence ; and I tell you quite plainly my determination. I demand of you my husband's address in England, and if you refuse to give it, I think it fair to warn you that I shall follow him to London by the next steamer; and once there, I shall have no difficulty in finding him.'

At the words 'I shall follow him,' Trenton Warren had started and left the door. He now turned abruptly to one of the windows, and stood there looking out, his face set and pale, for a full minute after she had concluded her slowly-delivered sentence.

When he turned to speak to her, she marked the whiteness of his face, and believed her threat had frightened him.

'I *cannot* give you your husband's address,' he said. 'I can write to him, and telling him that you are dissatisfied — as doubtless your own letters will convey— advise him to intrust you with the truth concerning his business in London in every respect. But no matter what you threaten, or what you do, I cannot, I will not, depart from his wishes in this matter.'

He slowly approached her, but did not pass round the table which stood between them; then suddenly seated himself, and studiously averting his eyes from her—indeed, Helen Griswold never caught his glance again during the remainder of the interview—he went on speaking in a dogged tone.

'I have made a blunder, Mrs. Griswold, and made a fool of myself! I cannot unsay what I have said, for it is true; the explanation of all the past which has offended you is the offence of the present. I have loved you, but I may cease to love you by an effort. A man does not go on loving with any kind of love very long if he is quite without hope; *and I am quite without hope.*'

The emphasis on these words would have conveyed a warning to the ear of a practised woman of the world; to Helen they conveyed merely an assurance, a relief, a mitigation of insult.

'Suppose,' he continued, 'we discuss the matter reasonably, not so much in

your interest or in mine, as in that of Griswold, your husband and my friend?'

'Your friend?'

'Yes, my friend. Women like you insist upon pushing everything to its extreme
verge; because I am not the soul of honour,
I must be a mere villain; because I love
you, I must, in every other sense and way,
be false to my friendship with your husband—a weak notion, a shallow judgment!
Accept my assurance that you are mistaken,
and let me go on. A total breach between
us will only make Alston suspicious and un-
happy, and, perhaps, morose. He is the
sort of man to suspect that a cool man
like me does not make love to a married
woman without something like encourage-
ment; another case of a weak notion and a
shallow judgment. But I will relieve you
of my presence. I will abandon the charge
laid upon me by Griswold, which you so
much resent, and he may never know it,
until time shall have changed everything,

enabled me to meet you with indifference, which has hitherto been impossible, and you to conquer your repugnance.'

In the evenness of his speech there was something artificial, which might have warned her had the temptation to snatch at the relief in his words been one whit less strong. But she heard no warning, only a blessed promise; only an indication that the cloud which had fallen upon her might be made to pass away, and leave a better and surer brightness than ever behind it.

'I will forgive, I will forget everything,' she said eagerly, and with a bright and beautiful blush, 'if you will go away and leave me; if you will never attempt to see me during Alston's absence. If I may be quite sure of that, and calculate upon it, I will never mention anything to him. It would be an awful pain to me to do so; it is an immense relief that you do not force me to tell it. I will send my letters through you;

I will ask you no question, if you will promise me, when you pass that door to-day, I shall see you no more until Alston has returned!'

'And I have come to my senses. The terms are hard, but I accept them. Only you forget, Mrs. Griswold, that you are exacting a very difficult thing from me; the relinquishment of my business, the placing it in the hands of other people, for at least the same term as that of Griswold's absence.'

'Why, would you leave New York?'

'How could I remain in New York and never come here, break through all my former habits, and neglect every recognition of Griswold, without being suspected of a motive; and from the suspicion of a motive to the discovery of its nature the interval is very, very short. No, I must leave New York, where lots of men know how I stand with Griswold, and have been seriously supposed to stand with you. I will do so; but in your turn you must promise me, in addition to your forgiveness, absolute silence towards Griswold.'

'Of course,' said Helen impatiently. 'I only care that he may never have the pain of knowing.'

'You mistake me again. I do not allude to that, but to my absence from New York. Men are too busy, and we signify too little to one another, for any risk to arise, or any one comparing notes with Griswold, when he comes back, about how long I have been away. But he must not be allowed to think that, for the sake of a mere pleasure trip—I should go to the Western States—I abandoned the charge he laid upon me, and broke the promise I made him at the last moment.'

'You are scrupulous enough in small matters,' thought Helen; but she only assented aloud again, impatiently.

'Then I have your promise, Mrs. Griswold, your positive assurance, that your letters to your husband shall contain no intimation whatever of my absence from New York?'

'They shall contain no mention of you whatever.'

'Pardon me, that will not do. Your correspondence with your husband is to be in journal form—you are right, it was not very delicate in him to tell any one anything of the kind—'

'I did not speak, sir.'

'True, there was no need of speech; but that journal, if it contains no mention of me, will be very unlike what Griswold expects.'

'I cannot help that. I can suppress all mention of you, but I cannot write letters about you, if that is the meaning you are aiming at. But you need not hesitate for that consideration. I shall merely have to remind my husband that we never agreed about you, and to say that I avoided on purpose the disagreeable subject.'

A momentary gleam of fury shot across

Warren's face; but he suppressed it, and made her a slightly artificial bow.

'This is agreed to, then,' he said; 'and so this interview, which had so stormy a beginning, ends peaceably. I am utterly beaten, Mrs. Griswold, acknowledging my defeat, and accepting the penalty. You will see me no more during Griswold's absence, and when we next meet the old things will have passed away.'

He bowed deeply and slowly, and walked out of the room with a quiet deliberate step; but there was something in his air, in his attitude, in his smile, as little like a beaten man as could be. When he had left the house—she waited, listening for the closing of the street-door—Helen Griswold lay back in her chair, and wept such bitter tears of anger, humiliation, and loneliness as her eyes had never before shed.

This terrible interview had terminated much better than she could have hoped. She had got rid of Warren, who would be powerless for the future to harm her, and she had avoided the necessity for wounding her husband. When he returned, she not only hoped that foreign travel and new acquaintances would have weaned him from his infatuation for Warren, but supplied him with a sounder standard whereby to measure his claim to regard. But where was the triumph which she ought to have felt at such a solution of the difficulty which had beset and harassed her whole married life? No signs of triumph came to the overwrought feelings and tired nerves; on the contrary, a strange kind of terror, depression, and misery settled down upon her, the more irresistible as she endeavoured to disentangle and sort the incidents of the interview which had just taken place. Her woman's instinct really aroused, and not wrong for once, told her the victory had been too easily won.

*　　*　　*　　*　　*

'So there is an end of my journal,' wrote

Helen the same night, when she was the only person awake under the roof. 'All my pretty and pleasant plans of setting down the inmost feelings of my heart, of recording them and every incident of the growth of my mind for Alston's eyes to see, are quite at an end. There is a secret in my life now which he must never know, and a dread within my breast which I cannot say to him that he might soothe it. How wretched they make me! how I detest them! Good heavens, how miserable one may be with everything beside one's-self to make one happy! I read over and over again the few pages I wrote this morning, and I ask myself, Can it be that I wrote them, and that since then I have learned so much of life, seen so much of human nature? That such treachery should exist as Trenton Warren's; that such credulity should exist as Alston's; that such blindness could be as mine! Thank God he has really promised to go away. I shall hardly breathe until he has gone, and I shall never stir beyond the door.   He said he would go at once.   How *am* I to write to Alston? The journal plan I must abandon; I feel that would now be impossible.   I must only just do one common every-day letter. Alston will not like it—he will reckon it as only one of my compromises.   No matter; it is a convenient excuse for faults far worse even than I have ever committed.'

CHAPTER VI.

A MYSTERIOUS COMMISSION.

BROWN-STREET, New York, is not a savoury locality. Although it is situated in the heart of the city, lying midway between the palatial splendour of the 'up-town' domestic residences and the enormous blocks of buildings forming the 'down-town' commercial establishments; though it runs parallel with, and at no great distance from, the famous Broadway; and though it has in its rear a magnificent square, where are to be found some of the grand old-fashioned roomy mansions which by their size and substantiality might well put the gimcrack erections of Fifth-avenue to the blush, yet is Brown-street a place of 'no 'count.'

The houses are for the most part two-storied buildings of the shabbiest description; the iron railings which should guard the 'stoop' or flight of steps leading to the doors are generally wanting, having been extracted feloniously for the purpose of sale, or broken up and converted into handy weapons of attack and defence by the Hibernian residents of the colony. The street-doors are but seldom closed, standing three or four inches open, but creaking furiously when further demands are made upon them, as though they had conceded all they meant to give; the windows of the first-floors are uniformly furnished with outside Venetian shutters, which, no matter what may be the time of year, are generally closed during the morning, while in the afternoon the passer-by can discern through them the half-dressed figures of frowsy women and girls, who have no scruple about entering into conversation or indulging in humorous repartee.

What the second-floor contained, none save those who have made their way into such penetralia (among which number I am not one) can say, but there is no doubt as to the purposes to which the underground cellars are applied. These are lager-beer saloons, dram-shops, whisky-stores, in some instances pretended billiard-halls or pistol-galleries, but in every case pandering to the vilest tastes of degraded humanity.

Stumble down these steep, broken, slippery steps and you stumble into Hades, you plunge head foremost into the infernal regions. Here, for the gratification of his countrymen, Max Heilbronn has opened a German gehenna, where Schinken and Blutwurst, dried and highly-seasoned Lachs, provoke the thirst of the Teutons, and induce them to wind up with something far stronger than the mild and insipid lager-beer with which they commence their potations. There Tim O'Dwyer, to insure the happiness of his compatriots, unfurled the green flag over the 'Ould Ireland' store,

strewed the stained and battered tables with
the latest received numbers of the *Bloody
Pike*, the *Patriot's Vitriol Bottle*, and other
cheerful publications, and provided a stock
of Bourbon and rye, after the consump-
tion of which his customers would clear the
floor and betake themselves to dancing jigs,
breaking heads, biting each other's noses
off, and other national pastimes.

The street itself, like the majority of the
streets of the sort in New York, is strewn
with garbage and refuse of every description; no need for its inhabitants to copy
the example of their more respectable neigh-
bours, and nightly put forth the barrow
filled with the cinders and sweepings of the
day; for what the Brown-street denizens
have to get rid of, they adopt a more easy
way with, and throwing it into the middle
of the street, there let it lie. The only one
portion of the road which is kept at all decent is the track of the horse-cars, which
enormous lumbering vehicles permeate a

portion of the street, and by their noise, the cracking of their drivers' whips, and the jangling of their bells attached to the horses, dispel some of the monotony which settles down on the neighbourhood during the daytime.

Some days after Trenton Warren's interview with Helen Griswold, and late in the afternoon, just when the early spring sun had withdrawn his brightness from the world, and the keen savage wind, sweeping through the wide thoroughfares, had reminded men that the reign of winter could scarcely be called at an end, a motley company was assembled in one of the Brown-street cellars, known to its frequenters as Naty Underwood's. A fat man Naty Underwood, with a round face and pendulous cheeks, little thin slits of eyes, and an upturned inquisitive nose; altogether not unlike a pig, whence probably the playful designation 'Porky' by which he is known to his familiars; a reserved man given to much quiet expectoration, a skilful concoctor of drinks, but always in a quiet manner, and as unlike the conventional idea of a 'bar-keeper' as possible.

Yet bar-keeping was Naty Underwood's trade, and by the exercise of it he lived. That dark smoke-discoloured saloon, whose original gaudily-stencilled walls now bore huge blots and stains, caused in some places by damp, in others by the sudden outburst of effervescent drinks, was his whisky-store; those long-necked labelled bottles on the wooden counter before him were his stock-in-trade, and the men lounging around were his customers.

Most of these latter, who belonged to that indescribable class of shabby-genteel people so common in New York—people who seem to have no recognised mode of living, who are thin, starved, and ragged, and yet always seem to have enough money to purchase a drink or to pay for a five-cent ride in the cars—most of these *habitués* of the saloon seem known to each other. At the end of the room, however, and just within the swing door by the bottom of the steps, was one who was evidently a stranger; a tall thin man, with a hard round glazed hat pressed down over a mass of tangled hair, and with a thick full beard. He was dressed in a rough short pea-jacket with huge horn buttons, and coarse blue-serge trousers, and looked like the second or third mate of an English collier. He sat with one hand leaning on the table and with his hat pulled well down over his eyes, but from time to time, from under the shade of its broad stiff brim, he looked sharply round at the assembled company as though he half anticipated interruption or attack, or glanced impatiently at the door as though expecting some one whose arrival had been unreasonably postponed.

Unquestionably, this stranger's appearance at Naty's aroused much curiosity amongst the ordinary frequenters of the saloon. There was a tendency amongst

them to resent what they considered in-
trusion, and a chance dropper-in to their
charmed circle; though this was a feeling
which found no favour with the host, who
was only desirous of increasing the number
of his guests; and on the present, as well as
on several previous occasions, sharp though
low muttered contentions had passed between him and them on the subject. Questions as to what the stranger might want
there, what a Johnny Bull was crowding
into those diggings for, and why Naty didn't
take upon himself to 'snake him out of
that,' were all met by the bar-keeper with
the reply that it was 'none of their business.'

A hint from long Abe Stevens that he
didn't pan out upon Johnny Bulls, and another from wiry Zeek Grimes that he didn't
freeze to dock wallopers, were also thrown
away upon Naty, and it seemed probable
that the landlord would have been called to
account even if the comfort of the guests
had not been interfered with, had not a clat-

tering on the steps and the swinging open
of the door diverted public attention.

These noises were followed by the entrance of a man who, after casting a rapid
glance round the room, and exchanging a
scarcely perceptible sign with the stranger
in the sailor's dress, walked up to the bar
amid universal signs of recognition and welcome, and clapped his long lean hand into
the fat moist palm of Naty Underwood.

A low blackguard-looking fellow this,
with his hang-dog air and the shifty furtive
glance out of his deep-set eyes; his cheeks
were thin and hollow, his unfringed lips
bloodless and closely set together; there
was nothing of the rough about his phy-
sique; no jowl or jaw or lowering cranium,
no bull neck; washed and decently dressed
he might have passed muster as an ordinary
citizen, but now his clothes were of anti-
quated cut and shiny with grease, his boots
broken and bulging, his battered hat stuck
on the top of his narrow thin head.   That

he was known to all, and popular as well, there could be little doubt, for the landlord gripped his hand with friendly warmth, and his entrance was received with cries of 'Hullo, Eph!' and 'Bully for you!' These salutations seemed rather to disconcert the new arrival, who glanced doubtingly to the corner where the sailor was seated; then, after ordering a hot whisky-punch, made his way towards him and took his seat beside him.

'You seem a powerful favourite here,' said the sailor sneeringly, in between his teeth. 'Bully for you and be hanged to it! What did you bring me here for? You knew I wanted to be quiet and unobserved; why did you name for our meeting this place, where you are apparently as well known as a nigger minstrel and as much thought of?'

The man was at first taken aback by this unexpected attack, but soon recovered himself.

'What place should I have named?' said he, in very much the same tone as the sailor had used. 'It is a pity I didn't propose to meet you at the Brevoort House, or in the hall of the Union Club; they would have been pleased to see me there, wouldn't they?' he added, glancing down at his clothes. 'I can't face the music right away, even if you can. I know this to be a safe and quiet place, where we can have our pow-wow in peace, and that is why I brought you here.'

There was something defiant in the air with which he regarded his companion across the table. Perhaps this was the influence of the whisky-punch, which had been brought to him while he was speaking, and of which he took a large gulp.

'Dry up,' said the sailor savagely; 'I don't want any more excuses. I told you to find a place where we could talk without having our conversation listened to, and you say you have done so in bringing me here.'

'And I repeat it,' said the man. 'There

was no possibility of your taking me to a respectable house, therefore it devolved upon me to bring you to a crib like this. I should not have proposed it,' he added, dropping his voice, ' if you had been in your old style, but like this'—and he laid his hand lightly on the sailor's rough pea-jacket—' it is right enough.'

'I don't see it,' said the sailor gruffly.

'You never do see anything unless it answers your own purpose,' said the man with a familiar laugh, ' and then it's astonish·ing how clear your sight becomes. This is how it is: You're a sailor, you see—may be mate of a liner—may be attached to one of the big steam companies—and you have got something you want to dispose of, something that you have not paid any duty on, perhaps something that has been handed over to you by a passenger who left the other side under a sort of cloud, and he could not conveniently move it ashore himself—you want to dispose of it as I say, and

Eph Jenkins has been recommended to you, and you have arranged to meet Eph Jenkins here; the boys round here know Eph, and will pretty soon guess that that is the sort of business you and he have together.'

'That is extremely satisfactory,' sneered the sailor, pushing back from his forehead some of the overhanging hair which seemed to inconvenience him, and gazing hard at his companion; 'you are still living the same kind of life then?'

'Did you expect me to have been made Secretary to the Treasury, or to have become mayor of New York?' asked the other.

'No,' said the sailor quietly, 'I didn't know but that even a greater change might have befallen you. I thought perhaps you might have become honest.'

'No,' said the man, with a short laugh, 'you didn't think that, or you would not have summoned me to do some work for you. Honest!' he cried, dropping his voice to a low hissing whisper, 'what have such as I, or you, for the matter of that, to do with honesty? I was honest once, but in those days I could have been of no service to you. It is only since I became the degraded brute I am that I fell within your clutches, was made your tool, and employed by you to do your dirty work.'

'For such, let me remark, you have been duly paid.'

'Paid!' cried the man. 'I have received money with which I have bought more whisky, in the hope of making myself drunk, and cheating myself into forgetfulness of the times when I was decent and respectable; money which has kept me from starving, and rendered me available for whatever you might order me to do.'

'Exactly,' said the sailor; 'you have a command of virtuous indignation which would obtain for you the greatest applause at the Bowery, Mr. Jenkins, and extort a perfect ovation of pea-nuts, but I confess you are to me most pleasing when practical. You have done work for me—dirty work you are pleased to call it—and have been paid for it, and how you spent your money was, of course, no affair of mine. Now, as I have already explained to you, I have some very important work to which you must devote your very best energies. If you carry it through successfully—and you are perfectly able to do so if you refrain from drink and one or two other little weaknesses—I shall make it my business to see that your future is provided for. If, on the contrary, by any negligence of yours you fail, I shall use such hold as I have over you in the opposite direction. You comprehend me?'

'Perfectly,' said the man, who had dropped his air of bravado ; 'what am I to do?'

'You have here,' said the sailor, taking from his inner breast-pocket a tolerably thick packet, 'a letter of instructions, written out in the fullest possible detail. There is nothing you can want to know that you will not find herein. I may, however, tell you at once, that the service I impose upon you requires you to leave New York; it may be many weeks before you are able to return. Under the circumstances, however, in which you are now situated,' he said, looking around him with an air of disgust, 'you will be rather pleased at the chance of getting away. It isn't a bad billet, you will find. You are to live like a gentleman among gentlemen, but it will require great discretion on your part, and especially abstinence from that;' and he lightly touched the empty glass on the table.

'I understand,' said Jenkins; 'and you may depend upon my being careful. And if I pull it off all right, you will keep to your promise?'

'You never knew me break my word yet, either in reward or punishment,' said the sailor. 'By the way, do you retain that old accomplishment, the exhibition of which on your part first brought us into contact—I mean the power of successfully imitating my handwriting?'

'I think so,' said Jenkins, hanging his head.

'That's right,' said the sailor; 'you may find it useful in this adventure. Now, as regards money. Here,' handing him a roll of dollar bills, 'is some to carry you on for the present. I don't at all imagine it will be enough, as you are by no means to stint yourself; and when you require more, you will find an address in the letter I have given you, to which you are to write for it. Be sure not to write to me, as I may probably be away from New York.'

'I understand,' said Jenkins, 'perfectly.'

'Then I don't think there is any reason for our stopping any longer in this delightful tavern,' said the sailor, rising.

When they reached the top of the steps

and were in the open street, he turned round, and giving Jenkins his hand, said:

'Good-night. Be sharp and prudent in this matter for your own sake. And, by the way, from that letter of instructions there is only one detail omitted — bear it well in mind. It is this: that when I direct you to go to Norfolk I shall mean Chicago.'

CHAPTER VII.

CONJUGAL CONFIDENCE.

BLEEKER-STREET is not attractive, either for rambling or residence. The tall houses present all the outward and visible signs of over-habitation with which eyes accustomed to exercise themselves in great cities are familiar, and the passage of the often-recurring tramways keeps up a perpetual vibration and a remorseless noise which banish all rest and peace for the sojourner. It is a street to live in only under pressure of necessity; and it is to be presumed that the people who do live in it have no great latitude for choice.

There are, however, degrees of discomfort, disorderliness, and out-of-elbow makeshift even in Bleeker-street, for the houses have numerous and desultory inmates, of all arms in the serried ranks of humanity fighting in the battle of life—only among the rank and file though, be it understood; and the parlours all along the line of the house fronts are mostly occupied by respectable artisans, with a sprinkling of superannuated *rentiers* in a small way.

An observer ascending from story to story would find the status of the dwellers in the monotonous dreary houses progressing crab fashion. The poorer in circumstances, the lower in position, the inmate, the higher up he, she, or they—or much more usually he and she and they—dwelt in the swarming buildings.

To Blecker-street Ephraim Jenkins took his way when his mysterious authoritative employer dismissed him; and one of the poorest, dingiest, and most crowded of its houses received his somewhat slouching form. His form was a little less slouching than when he had struggled down to the place of rendezvous to meet the sailor ; the most inveterate loafer pricks up for a little while under the proud consciousness of having got something to do for which he is going to be paid.

Ephraim Jenkins did not object to a temporary occupation of a kind to leave him a future margin of idleness, without danger of coming to want; and it was with a decided accession of cheerfulness to his countenance and alacrity to his step that he climbed the stair of one of the least inviting of the houses in Bleeker-street to the topmost story, and presented himself in a dull, close, ill-furnished room, carpetless, curtainless, and forlorn-looking. This room had one tenant already—a woman, who sat in an attitude expressive of deep despondency and utter listlessness beside the rusty stove, leaning her head against the wall, and with her hands folded in her black stuff apron.

This woman moved when Ephraim Jenkins entered; but before her glance turned towards him it fell upon an object, common-

place in itself, but to which that unconscious spontaneous look lent a pathetic interest; it was an empty cradle. The woman
was still young, and though not quite handsome, was very comely. She had kindly
bright dark eyes, black hair, a fresh colour,
and a singularly honest expression of countenance. She was neatly though poorly
dressed, in what seemed to be an attempt
at mourning, but wore no new article of
attire; though it was evident the motive of
the attempt was recent, for when she spoke
to Jenkins, it was with streaming eyes and
a broken voice.

'What a time you have been away, and
how lonely I have felt!' she said, as he
hung his hat on a nail, and threw himself
heavily into one of the two chairs in the
room.

'Yes, Bess, I've been a goodish bit
about it; but it's been worth it,' he replied;
'the tide's on the turn, my girl, and we
shall do well now.'

'It's turned too late for me, then. O, Eph, to think it was only yesterday we buried him! It seems like a year of misery.'

The empty cradle had a melancholy meaning. This woman's infant had suddenly sickened and died three days before, and one of the repetitions, countless as human lives, of the human tragedy was going on in that shabby room in Bleeker-street. The woman would not be comforted, because the child was not.

'Poor little Ted!' said Jenkins, with an awkward tenderness of a man honestly endeavouring to soothe a grief which he does not share, and hardly comprehends. 'I daresay it is much better for him; but it's hard on you, Bess, considering how fond you were of him, and how you never grudged the trouble; but he'd never have been well, you know. Even our turn of luck couldn't have straightened his little legs or strengthened his little back; and you would only have fretted worse to see him growing up not able to get along for himself.'

'That's true, Eph ; but I can't think about it now,' said the woman with an impatient shiver, as she rose and dried her eyes. 'I would rather have "the trouble," as you call it, and him, than any luck you can tell me of without him.'

'Of course, of course,' assented Ephraim; 'and you must not think I don't miss him too, Bess. Children ain't as much to men as they are to women, because men have so much more to think of.' Mr. Jenkins's *bonâ-fide* belief in his own occupied mind and industrious life was something edifying to behold, not to say humorous. 'And you know, Bess, you're a deal more to me than any children could ever be, and I can't bear to see you fretting.'

She had begun to lay out some teathings in a noiseless tidy way, and he drew his chair to the table with a not unskilful assumption of wanting his tea. Ephraim

Jenkins was loose and a loafer, but he was not more than 'half bad,' and the other half was redeemed by a very genuine and constant love for his wife. She saw the best side of his character always, and she formed an extremely erroneous estimate, happily for her, of the whole of it.

'While the tea is drawing, I will tell you all about it, Bess,' he said; and she sat down quietly, looking straight at him, and evidently trying hard to rally her spirits and fix her attention. 'I thought it was only a temporary job to buy a horse at some Western fair, or to go and look at some premises, or to follow up some debtor,' began Jenkins; 'and I was not a little stumped when I found that Warren wanted me for a big job and some time—three months certain, Bess.'

'Three months! What for?'

'Well, that's it. I don't exactly know what for. At least, I know what I've got to do, but I don't know what it means;

however, it's no business of mine, as you'll
see.'

Thereupon Ephraim Jenkins proceeded
to give his wife an account of the interview
between himself and Warren. It was a
garbled account, and it presented the mission he had undertaken in a light which he
perfectly well knew was not its real one;
but he had an elastic conscience, and was
apt to accommodate circumstances to his
wife's notions when they differed from his
own, rather than to abide by the cold, un-
yielding, and inconvenient letter of facts.
He made out to her that he was to be employed as an agent, not as a substitute; for
he had an instinctive consciousness that she
would take alarm at the other view of the
transaction, and discern the existence of in-
definite danger in the very evident trickery
which it implied. He did not propose to
himself to give so very free a version of the
transaction as he found himself led into
giving, but the fact was, that when he had

concluded what he called an 'account' of
the interview from which he had just returned, his wife had only two clear ideas
about it—the first that he was going to
leave her for he did not exactly know how
long, the second that he was going to conduct certain business operations of a kind
with which she had no reason at all to believe him practically acquainted. She was
not an educated woman, but neither was
she ignorant, and it struck her as a most
unaccountable imprudence that a man of
business should put affairs into the hands
of a person who had neither knowledge nor
position to bring to the transaction of them.

Ephraim Jenkins perceived at once that
his story had not satisfied his wife, and that
he must improve upon it if he hoped to
serve the first important end to be gained,
i.e. her willing acquiescence in their inde-
finite separation.

'Whatever I shall tell her'—so ran the
ingenuous current of his thoughts—'I must

not let out that I am going to pass for an independent gentleman, for, of course, she would like to have her share in a game of that kind, and why shouldn't she?'

'I don't understand it plain enough yet, Eph,' she said; and Eph knew the resolute ring in the voice, quite free from temper, but meaning him to mind it. 'You must be more distinct, please. And I should like you to tell me how it is that you and this Warren have turned friends again. I never knew much about your quarrel or how you were mixed up with him at first; but it seems to me, considering he wouldn't answer your letters or see you or help you to get anything to do for some time back, he must have some very strong reason for changing round all of a sudden, and putting you into a thing which must want manage-ment and must mean confidence.'

'Ain't she shrewd!' thought Jenkins rather admiringly, though his wife's shrewd-ness bothered him just then; 'goes straight at it and hits it in the bull's-eye.' And then he formed a resolution.

'You are quite right, Bess,' he replied. 'I am sure his reason is a very strong one, only I don't know it, and it don't matter to me, for I am safe to get paid, and you see that's the chief thing, and I'm sure you'll allow—and there's the queerest tricks going on in business, tricks that would make you stare to hear of and you could hardly believe. If there is any such tricks up in this game, you understand, it's Warren will be playing them, not me, and they don't concern me; and you may take your oath Warren knows what he's about. But I am going to tell you something, Bess, which I have not told you before, just because we have always had enough trouble to get along, and a big share of it has been yours, my girl, and I did not want to make it bigger by giving things a look of greater hardship and blacker injustice than they need have; but I can't go on without tell-

ing you now, Bess, when you ask me how
it comes that Warren has changed his mind
and his hand about me. You know he is
not aware of your existence!'

'Yes,' Bess replied anxiously, 'I know
you thought it better he should not know
you were married.'

'I had my reasons. Long ago, Warren
said to me he would never get me another
job, or help me with another cent, if I
mixed myself up in any affair with a woman. I have no doubt he did not mean by
that if I married, for he never thought of
such a thing, but he just said that, and he
meant it. "He would not have any woman
told anything about his affairs," he said,
"and I had better act on the caution."
did, Bess, *you* know how, and I have been
obliged to stick to it. If I had gone to him
and pleaded poor little Ted, instead of soft-
ening him, the notion of the poor little
crippled baby would only have exasperated
him, and he would have told me I was a

cursed fool, and might take the consequences. It was only while he believed me to be knocking about alone, and at his beck and call, that I could count on Warren's remembering me sometimes for his own sake; and so I never told him I had a wife, Bess, and I can't tell him now; but I will when this job is through, for I mean to save every cent I can while it is on, and then we will set up in some little way, and I will be steady.'

Poor Bess had heard many such promises already during the two years she had been Ephraim Jenkins's wife, and had tested their worthlessness, but she still cherished the delusion concerning her husband, which, however foolish, is always lovable and excusable in a woman; and therefore she smiled, faintly indeed, for the little tenant had left its cradle empty too lately for the mother's lips to smile in full or genuinely, and said, 'I know you will, Eph; I know you will.'

'That's hearty, my girl, and encourages a man. I will say for you, Bess, you never do nag, not even in your own mind, you know. I know you don't, for I should see it in your face if you held your tongue ever so. And now for what I promised to tell you. There is a reason why Warren should help me, why he should turn round after all his hardness and put a job into my hands rather than into any one else's; for he is my brother, Bess; yes, indeed, my father was his father, but his mother was his father's wife, and my mother was that wife's maid—that's all the difference! Only a trifle!' he added, with a bitter laugh, 'but it made a deuced deal of difference to me. My father's wife died when Warren and I were young children, and we grew up together in a rather indecent sort of fellowship, I daresay—he in the parlour, and I in the stable-yard; but we were never long parted, and there has always been some sort of feeling—a bad sort generally on his side—between us. I have been a loafer and a ne'er-do-well; it is not elevating and encouraging to have such a family history as mine to look back upon; though, mind, I don't mean to lay the blame on that, Bess; that's cant, and cowardly too! Now you know all about it, and you understand why Warren, when he wants some one to help him and to keep it dark, sends for me.'

'Yes, I understand that now, and a good many other things as well,' said Bess, 'and I do hope, Eph, you will get free of him by this job, and let us make a fair start. But what am I to do? I must try to get some plain sewing, I suppose, and stay here, unless I can get a cheaper place!'

'Plain sewing be hanged!' exclaimed Ephraim, slapping the rickety table with his hand and making the cracked crockeryware ring; 'you sha'n't go in for *that*. I've got a notion, Bess, and I think you will like it. You know what the doctor said, don't you, about poor little Ted's death, and your having to be careful on account of leaving off nursing so suddenly?'

Bess nodded; her eyes filled with tears.

'Well, then'—he spoke with a little effort, creditable to the poor loafer—'look here,' taking a newspaper from his pocket, 'here's an advertisement for a wet-nurse. "Wanted immediately, by Mrs. Alston Griswold, of Fifth-avenue, a young woman to undertake the charge of a delicate infant." What do you say to trying for the place at once? for I must leave you to-morrow, Bess; it's hard lines, but Warren must have his dollar's worth for his dollar; it will be a good one, I'm sure, and if you were to get it, my mind would be at rest about you.'

'O, Eph, to have a child at my breast, and little Ted in his grave!' cried the young mother, with a burst of infinitely touching sorrow, and threw her arms around the 'loafer's' neck.

He let her cry in silence for a few moments, and then she recovered herself, and said:

'This is foolish, I know. The idea is a good one, Eph; but I don't think it can be done. Do you know anything about Mrs. Griswold?'

'No, I don't,' said Jenkins, with an odd look, which his wife did not observe; 'but where's the difficulty? The advertisement is only this morning's, and you might see after the place to-night.'

'No lady would take me without a recommendation, and where am I to get one?'

'O, for the matter of that,' said Jenkins incautiously, 'I'll write you out half-a-dozen different ones in half-a-dozen different hands; and the last lady you lived with can be gone to Europe, so that she can't be applied to.'

One of Mr. Jenkins's accomplishments

was a faculty for writing several different hands, which Bess never liked, though she had hitherto regarded it with only a vague disfavour and distrust. But she coloured violently when Jenkins said this, and hastily bade him:

'Hush, hush! you are only jesting, and I don't like such jests. No; I will go to this lady, and try if she will engage me when I tell her the truth about our little Ted.'

*   *   *   *   *

Bess Jenkins put on her mourning bonnet and shawl—the only new articles of attire in her scanty wardrobe—and the two set off to walk to Fifth-avenue. On the way Jenkins confided to his wife—being forced to do so in order that she might be able to write to him during his absence—that condition of his undertaking which he had been most strenuously cautioned against revealing: his assumption of the name of Warren. Bess was vaguely alarmed when she heard it, and when he told her she must let no one see the address upon her letters; but she felt that remonstrance was now useless, and so she submitted.

CHAPTER VIII.

A WANDERING STAR.

IN that tall square block of buildings known as Vernon-chambers, Piccadilly, a London bachelor must be fastidious indeed if he cannot, no matter what his tastes may be, find a residence to suit him.

There are suites of rooms, easy of access and commanding enormous rents, and there are single apartments, so loftily situate that they look down upon Buckingham Palace in the distance, which can be had for a small sum—that is to say, a comparatively small sum when the situation and accommodation are taken into consideration.

The advantages of a residence in Vernon-chambers are great and manifold. It is a great thing for a young man new to the metropolis, and just commencing his career in diplomacy, law, or commerce—for commerce has been found to pay, and is now quite as fashionable as any of the learned professions—to be enabled to put ' Vernon-chambers' on his card, it being a recognised address amongst those dinner-and-ball-giving members of society, the cultivation of whose good will is so necessary to the well-being of all young men.

Then, again, it is in the most desirable quarter of the town; handy to the clubs and to the park; within a shilling fare of all the theatres; and yet providing its inhabitants—those who dwell in the topmost stories at all events—with plenty of fresh air; and the pleasant expanse of the Green-park to look upon, instead of the dismal line of brick or stucco abomination on which most Londoners are compelled to feast their eyes when they come to the window in ungratified search for light and air.

It is probable, however, that none of these considerations figured as inducements in the mind of Mr. Bryan Duval, when, some three years before the period of our story, he took a set of rooms on the second floor, and agreed, without hesitation or attempt at abatement, to pay for them the rather stiff price of three hundred a year.

Mr. Duval did not go much into fashionable society; but at such great houses as he was in the habit of frequenting in the season he would have been as welcome if he lived in Greek-street, Soho—a choice locality, in which, indeed, at some anterior period of his life, he had once pitched his tent. He was not a member of any club, and he would as soon have thought of going into the Thames as into the park; he hated fresh air (his first order in connection with his new rooms was to have double windows made to exclude the noise), and if he occasionally looked out on the Green-park, it was not with any idea of pleasing his eyes with its verdure, or amusing himself with contemplating what was going on there, but rather in a fit of abstraction, when he had got into what he had called 'a knot' in the work on which he was engaged, and during the disentanglement of which he would, perhaps, lean his forehead against the window, and stare straight out before him, with a prolonged gaze, which saw nothing.

It was not to be imagined, however, that Mr. Duval had selected this residence haphazard; he had a motive for everything he did; and, when it suited him, was ready to explain it in the most candid manner.

'I took these rooms,' he would say to any inquiring friend, 'and I pay about twice what they are really worth, because I wanted them. My business lies sometimes in Bayswater, and sometimes in Basinghall-street' —he would smile grimly as he pronounced the last name—'and I want to be right in the centre, "the hub of the wheel," as they say in America, whence I can fly out east or west with equal ease. Then again, of late years, a certain number of swells, not being

able to spend their money quickly enough
on the turf, have chosen to mix themselves
up with my profession, and this is a handy
kind of place to come and see me at when
they want. I have not any feeling for them
but one of intense contempt; but that, of
course, I keep to myself. Out of them I
get a certain portion of my bread-and-cheese,
and so I treat them civilly enough, never
rubbing them the wrong way, never bowing
down and worshipping them. Then, again,
I want large rooms, for there are books and
papers, and files of playbills, and all sorts of
things knocking about; and there is a little
slip of a room out there—the warm-bath, I
call it—where my secretary works; and altogether the crib suits me, and is not so
bad.'

The ' crib,' as Mr. Duval called it in his
pleasant *argot*, was furnished and fitted with
such good taste that it might have puzzled
an ingenious Sybarite to suggest an im-
provement in it.

It has been said that the arrangement of a room often furnishes an index to the owner's mind; and if there be truth in the dictum, Mr. Bryan Duval must be a singular compound of many apparently antagonistic qualities.

The broad, cosy-cushioned, spring-seated ottoman, or divan, in green and gold, which ran the whole length of one side of the room, was counter-balanced by three or four grave, high-backed, Puritan-looking chairs, in the darkest of brown leather; a huge, massive black oak writing-table, littered all over with papers, proof-sheets, and bills, had its pendant in an elegant sandalwood davenport, inlaid with mosaic, on which lay a green velvet blotting-book, with raised crest and monogram. The wall opposite to the ottoman was taken up by a large black oak bookcase, and among the treasures which filled it, and overflowed on to the floor, were rare elzevirs in creamy vellum covers, British classics in stout old leather jackets, a splendid edition of French plays—ancient and modern—rare works on costume splendidly illustrated, novels of the day, bluebooks, political pamphlets, two or three thick rolls of Irish ballads bought in Dublin streets, French pasquinades, and comic songsters. A great roaring double breechloader, by Lancaster, hung close over the head of an ancient arquebuse, the stock of which was elegantly inlaid with pearl and ivory, and on the writing-table a gold-hilted dagger—said to have been worn by Henry of Navarre—lay side by side with a very vicious-looking six-shooter, with an inscription on its barrel: 'Jacob F. Bodges and Co., Danville, Pa.'

Nor was the room without examples of art; a wonderfully executed copy of Greuze's 'La Cruche Cassée' hung in the place of honour, proof engravings after Sir Joshua Reynolds and Landseer occupied every available space on the walls, and in a recess, half shaded by deep-green velvet curtains, was a marvellous Venus, by Pradier. But, *en revanche*, the mantelpiece was studded with Danton's comic caricatures of celebrities, and on the wall, suspended by the frame of Sir Joshua's 'Strawberry Girl,' which overlapped it, was a flaring-coloured lithograph of Pat Hamilton, in his favourite character of Bryan Boroo, with on it a memorandum, in Mr. Duval's own hand: 'Wants situation in third act altered; address Wolverhampton till 29th.'

On a fine morning in early spring the occupant of these rooms stood with his back to the fireplace, where—for the cold winds had not yet abated—some logs were burning on the iron dogs, with an open letter in his hand.

Mr. Bryan Duval was a man of middle size, with small, clear-cut, regular features, and large, dark, melancholy eyes; his soft dark hair was parted in the middle, and taken back behind his ears; his moustaches and imperial were long, and carefully trained

—there were times when the exigencies of his profession required that these luxurious appendages should be shaved off, and then, though he was far too conscientious in his art not to sacrifice to it his personal vanity, Mr. Duval mourned and refused to be comforted.

He was gorgeously dressed in a loose jacket and trousers of violet velvet, his small shirt collar, turned down over the deep crimson necktie, was clasped at his throat with a diamond stud, and on the little finger of his small white right hand he wore a massive gold signet ring, engraved with a viscount's coronet of the Duvals, of which great family he always stated his father was a scion.

As Mr. Duval read the letter attentively, which was stamped with a coronet and a large initial L, he brushed away with his hand the wreaths of blue smoke from his cigar, which interfered with its proper perusal, and shook his head slowly.

'It won't do, my dear Laxington,' he muttered, half aloud; 'it really cannot be thought of. It is all very well for you to say that you will stand the racket, that I shall not be liable for a penny, and shall only have to give my name; but you don't appear to understand that that is the exact commodity which is more valuable to me than anything else! It is solely on the strength of my name that I hold my position. I cannot afford to be connected with failure, and failure—and dead failure—it undoubtedly will be, if your lordship proposes to take the Pomona, in order that little Patty Calvert may play leading parts! What a wonderful thing it is,' continued Mr. Duval, throwing down the letter, and plunging his hands into his trousers pockets, 'to see a man in Laxington's position so eager for such an affair as this! I don't think, if I had been born a peer of the realm, with a couple of hundred thousand a year, and vast family estates, that I should have cared to go into management. I imagine I could have filled up my time in a better way than that, and made a good thing of it too. Good heavens, what a taste! To smell gas and orange-peel, to be pushed about by carpenters and supers, to be estimated a nincompoop, and to have to pay a couple of hundred a week for the pleasure! Let me see,' he continued, taking up the letter, ' "clear half the receipts, no risk, only give your name. Think of it, and let me know. Yours sincerely, Laxington." No, I think not. Very affectionate, but it won't do. There is no part in any piece of mine which little Patty could attempt to touch, and I have no time to write one for her; so we shall have to fall back upon burlesques and breakdowns and Amazons in their war paint, and that kind of thing, which would not suit my book at all. Besides, that little door, just by the opposite prompt private box, going between the house and the stage, would be always on the swing, and we should have H.R.H.'s and foreign ambassadors, and Tommy This of the Life Guards, and Billy That of the Garrick Club, always tumbling about behind the scenes. I don't think I would entertain it if I were free; but with this American business on hand, it is not worth thinking of a second time, and so I will tell L. at once.'

He touched a handbell as he spoke, and a gray-haired keen-looking man presented himself at the door.

' Good-morning, Mr. Marks,' said Duval. ' Come in, pray. You have brought your usual budget with you, I perceive,' pointing to a bundle of letters which the secretary held in his hand; ' anything of importance?'

' No, sir,' replied Mr. Marks, ' not of any particular importance. Price, the manager of the Alexandria at Ruabon, offers ten shillings a night for the *Cruiskeen Lawn* for a week certain.'

' Does he!' interposed Mr. Duval, smiling

and showing all his white teeth; 'and he has the impudence to call himself "Price." Of course, no!'

'I have written so, sir,' said Mr. Marks. 'They want the music for *Anne of Austria* at Durham, and the plot of the scenery for *Varco the Vampire* at Swansea. I have sent the usual note to the Sunday papers announcing that *Pickwick's Progress* will be put into rehearsal at the Gravity on Monday. By the way, sir, will you allow me to suggest that that name has been used before?'

'What name, my dear Mr. Marks?' said Bryan Duval, looking up with an affectation of the greatest innocence.

'Pickwick, sir,' said Mr. Marks; 'Mr. Dickens has a work in which that name occurs.'

'Ah,' said Mr. Duval, stroking his silky moustache, 'by the way, now you mention it, I think he has—curious that that idea did not occur to me before. However, this is *Pickwick's Progress*, and I don't think Mr. Dickens or Mr. Anybodyelse has ever had anything of that sort; at all events, I am clear they can say nothing about infringement of copyright, so we will hold to *Pickwick's Progress*, Mr. Marks. Anything else?'

'A newspaper, sir, from Melbourne, evidently sent by Mr. Prodder.'

'Prodder,' repeated Mr. Duval, closing his eyes; 'ah, I remember — the stage-struck pork-butcher. Yes, and what of Prodder?'

'He seems to have made a great success with Romeo, sir; the paper says he quite hit the taste of the Melbourne audience.'

'Ah, that is not very complimentary to the Melbourne audience, is it, Marks? However, anything more?'

'Yes, sir, a letter from Mr. Van Buren, acknowledging the receipt of your signed copy of the engagement, saying he will take your rooms at the Hoffman House, and either he or Mr. Jacobs will be at the Cunard wharf when the Cuba comes in.'

'Good,' said Bryan Duval, slowly rubbing his hands together. 'Van Buren is a man of business. That engagement is going to turn up trumps, Marks, and my old friends, the Yankees, are going to do me another good turn. By the way, any reply from Miss Montressor?'

'Yes, sir,' said Mr. Marks, 'this,' touching a small pink note. 'She will be here at eleven, precisely.'

'That with a woman means half-past twelve,' said Duval, nodding his head. 'All right. Now be good enough to write a letter for my signature in reply to this from Lord Laxington—polite, of course, but giving no loophole, saying that I should have been delighted, &c., but that I have made other arrangements which prevent the possibility—you understand. You may mention that I am going to America—no, on second thoughts we must let the newspapers have that information first; they would be wild if it leaked out through private sources.'

Mr. Marks bowed and retired to the warm-bath, Bryan Duval lit another cigar, threw himself on the divan, and taking out a small gilt-edged memorandum-book, began looking through its leaves, and scratching a few figures upon them. 'That's it,' he said to himself after a pause. 'I have three hundred and eighty pounds in the bank now. *Pickwick's Progress*, if it makes anything like a hit, will probably be good for thirty pounds a night—let's say sixty; then before I sail, the returns from the provinces for *Anne of Austria*, *Varco the Vampire*, and the *Cruiskeen Lawn*—the idea of that fellow wanting it for ten shillings a night—ought to bring me eighty pounds—eighty! O, more—let's say two hundred and eighty. I should think that that must be something like a thousand pounds that I ought to take away with me. Then Van Buren's Varieties

holds three thousand people at a dollar each
—three thousand dollars are six hundred
pounds—but the exchange will probably
have risen by the time I get there—let
us call it eight hundred. It costs them to
pull up the curtain two hundred dollars a
night. I will make an alteration there, however—great reduction—let's call it seventy
dollars. Seventy as against three thousand
—let me see,' said Bryan Duval, slowly
pulling at his imperial, 'I think I must
bring back to England in three months'
time at least ten or twelve thousand
pounds—'

His calculations were cut short by a
whistle from a mouth-piece in the wall, to
which he applied his ear; immediately an-
swering with the words: 'Show her up.'
'Miss Montressor below, eh?' he muttered,
repeating the information which had been
given him through the pipe. 'Now, I think
I have got a card in Miss Montressor, if I
only handle her rightly.'

He opened a door of communication with his dressing-room, disappeared for a moment, and returned with his hair fresh brushed, and a scented handkerchief peeping out of his jacket pocket. Then he stepped on to the staircase, and, as Miss Montressor reached the landing, he took her by both hands and led her into the room.

Miss Clara Montressor was a woman of about six-and-twenty, not tall, but what Mr. Duval called ' a good stage height,' not stout, but well developed. Her features were anything but faultless, yet her face, as a whole, was very pretty, and her expression quite charming. She had long lustrous eyes, which, whether they were green or gray, no one had ever been able to determine. Lord Alicampayne of the Life Guards said they were ' bwight blue,' but Miss Theresa Colombo of the T.R.D.L., whose salary was two pounds a week less than Miss Montressor's, and who did not get half so many

bouquets, said they were 'cat's eyes.' Her
nose was a little retroussé, but she had
rich pouting lips, sound small white teeth,
and her complexion was such as you only
see on a peach, or on a lady who uses
Poudre à la Bismuth, dite Veloutine. Her
hair, which was one of her chief attractions,
was gold-brown, and she had had the sense
not to attempt to change its colour. Altogether, Miss Montressor was a very nice-
looking person, and very becomingly
dressed.

So Mr. Bryan Duval thought, as he
seated her on the divan and took up his
position in one of the high - backed arm-
chairs in front of her. Mr. Duval's thoughts
about his present visitor, and indeed about
most ladies, were wholly professional—his
time was too valuable to be taken up with
flirtation, and he had a free and-easy manner with him which, while it was very
agreeable, obviously meant nothing.

'It was very good of you to come here

this morning, Miss Montressor,' he commenced, sitting back and waving his scented
pocket-handkerchief gently in the air—it
was excellent Ess. Bouquet, and he knew
that Patchouli and Jockey Club were about
Miss Montressor's mark.

'It was very good of you to send for
me, Mr. Duval,' said Miss Montressor, without the slightest embarrassment, 'and I was
very glad to come—putting aside any question of business—I was anxious to see what
you were like without any make-up.'

'Well,' said Duval, jumping up from his
seat and striking an attitude, 'and how do
you find me?'

'O, exactly the same,' replied the visitor; 'there is no mistaking those raven locks
and those spikes,' drawing her finger across
her upper lip. 'You are not like old Frank-
lin, who is quite black, or rather quite blue,
at night, and a lively piebald—like a horse
in a circus—when he comes to rehearsal in
the morning. O, it must be delightful to be

made love to by you, more especially after a fortnight's Juliet to Hedger's Romeo, and Mr. Hedger always will take his supper between the acts, and he is so partial to spring onions.'

'Horrible Hedger!' cried Duval, throwing up his hands; 'my taste in that line, my dear, don't go beyond the slightest *soupçon* of garlic, and I religiously deny myself that when I am acting. One great fault of our English actors is that they know nothing of the delicacies of the *cuisine.*'

'O, but you do, and you are yourself a most wonderful cook. I know all about that,' she cried, clapping her hands. 'I heard it from a Mr. Foster, an American gentleman whom I was introduced to the other day, and who knew you when you first went out to New York.'

'Ah, by the way, I had a letter from Foster last night. He told me he had met you, and sent you a rather jolly message, which I will deliver to you later on.'

'Why not now?'

'Pleasure after business, my dear.   I never do anything until the business which I am transacting is out of hand. By the way, will you have a glass of sherry? You can sip that and talk business at the same time.'

'I think I will, please,' said Miss Montressor simply; 'and is there a biscuit anywhere about?   I am awful hungry.'

'Awfully hungry, my dear Clara,' said Bryan Duval, touching her arm lightly with his finger; 'awfully, not awful—adverb, not adjective—don't mind my telling you, do you, dear? These little slips, you know, are awkward in public. A biscuit? Hundreds! thousands! and something better than a biscuit—look here!'

He darted into the ante-room and speedily returned with a silver waiter, covered with a white cloth, which he placed before her.

'Plovers' eggs, my dear Clara,' he cried,

handing her a plate; 'shilling apiece in Covent-garden. I tell you the price, not to stint you, but to tickle your appetite — Vienna bread from Popowaski's, the man in the Quadrant; country butter just out of the refrigerator; Oloroso sherry, and a bottle of Brighton seltzer. One, two, three, and you're off.'

'What a ridiculous fellow you are!' said Miss Montressor, with a plover's egg between her pretty, jewel-laden fingers. 'I have always thought of you as a suffering lover, the fiery Raoul, the heart-broken Edgar, but here, at home, you are as jolly as a sandboy.'

'That's because I have to be so uniformly miserable on the stage, my dear,' said Mr. Duval, taking some choice loose tobacco out of the drawer, and rolling up a *papelito*, 'and one cannot be always doing the water-cart business. Are the plovers' eggs good?'

'Divine.'

'And the Oloroso?'

'Delicious—quite a nutty flavour.'

'O, don't,' cried Bryan Duval, putting up his hand, 'that is out of the advertisement of the Standard Sherry. However, I am glad you like it; and now to business. You have considered my proposition?'

'I have.'

'And you agree to it?'

'Provided the terms suit me; you were to mention them at this meeting.'

'Wisest of females,' said Bryan, puffing a cloud of blue smoke through his nose, and watching it waft away, 'so I was! I don't think there will be any difficulty about them —sixty pounds a week, and half a clear benefit in every town where we stop a fortnight.'

Miss Montressor threw her egg-shell into the plate, wiped her dainty fingers on the napkin, and said, in a deep tragic voice:

'Selim, take me. I am yours!'

'Here,' cried Bryan Duval, in very deep chest notes, 'here and hereafter—ha! ha! cue for prompter to ring for trap. Then we may look upon that as settled.'

'That's so, colonel,' said Miss Montressor, with a slight nasal intonation; 'they are all colonels out there, are they not?'

'There is my hand upon it—tip us your flipper,' cried Bryan Duval; and after shaking hands with his visitor, he hitched up his trousers and danced a few steps of the hornpipe round the room. 'Marks shall draw up the agreement, and we will have it properly signed and sealed. I will let you know the date of sailing, but you had better get ready at once. O, by the way, Foster's message.'

'O yes! what was it?' cried Miss Montressor eagerly.

'Foster is one of those Americans who, when they crawl out of the commercial shell in which they are engaged all day, find no such pleasure, no such thorough change, as the theatre affords them. He is over here on commercial matters, but he is mad about theatricals; and he is going to give a dinner at Richmond on Sunday, and he wants you to go.'

Miss Montressor hesitated for a moment. She had certain relations, of which no one but herself and those in her immediate household were aware, and she wondered whether these 'relations' would prove a hindrance to her accepting the invitation.

Bryan Duval saw the look in her face, and had a vague idea of what she was pondering over—vague, but still an idea—he had known so many Miss Montressors in his life.

'Don't hesitate,' he said; 'don't make any mistake about it; it is going to be a tremendously jolly party; lots of people you know—fellows in the Guards, and fellows on the press, and a good dinner, and no end of fun. Say "yes."'

'I will,' said Miss Montressor. 'You

can tell Mr. Foster I shall be delighted to come.'

'Right,' said Bryan Duval. 'Then I will drive you down. I will tool my chestnuts up to the villa at four P.M. precisely.'

Miss Montressor stepped into her neat little brougham in a very complacent state of mind. She had long wished to be a star, but her chances in this hemisphere had not been great. Here was a fulfilled ambition, accompanied, indeed, with certain difficulties, which, however, the lady felt disposed to treat philosophically as mere points of detail. She had time to make up her mind as to her mode of action on a certain complex line very near her hand before the brougham stopped at the unpretending entrance to her very pretty abode at Brompton. She rather expected to find Mr. Dolby waiting for her, and her first question to her maid was whether he had yet arrived. The answer was in the affirmative, so she went straight into the drawing-room, where she found Mr. Dolby occupied in patiently examining the contents of a photograph-book, with which he had been long familiar. Miss Montressor skilfully assumed a tone, not only of satisfaction, but of girlish elation, as she ran forward, exclaiming: 'Isn't it delightful? It's all settled!'

Mr. Dolby closed the photograph-book, replaced it on the table, and looked up at her. There was no elation nor delight in his countenance as he said: 'Are you alluding to the engagement?'

'Of course I am. What else do you suppose I was talking about?'

'I did not presume to guess. You are extravagantly delighted or inconceivably distressed, in the wildest spirits or in the depths of despair, so frequently, for causes which my incomplete male understanding is incapable of discerning, that I did not know whether it might be a question of a

new trimming, or an exchange of dogs between you and Miss Campbell, which had
produced that very becoming animation to
which you have not treated me lately.'

'O,' said Miss Montressor, 'you are out
of temper. You were yesterday, you know,
and you have not got over it. How I hate
men who keep up spite! I have a great
mind not to tell you anything that has occurred to-day.'

'I should be aghast at the threat if I
did not know by experience that you are
what you call "dying to tell me;" whereas
I am quite willing to hear, and I can therefore wait,' said Mr. Dolby.

All this was rather trying, and calcu-
lated to damp the high spirits with which
Miss Montressor had returned; but she was
accustomed to the acerbity of Mr. Dolby's
humour, and she made light of it. 'What
an unpleasant man he would be as a husband!' she often thought in her odd frank
way. 'I would not be his wife for any con-

sideration; he would bully any one he could not get away from awfully.'

This familiar reflection passed through her mind on the present occasion; but it did not impair the cheerfulness of her countenance, or the glee in her voice, as she proceeded in a rather chattering style to repeat to Mr. Dolby the particulars of her interview with Bryan Duval, and to dilate upon the thorough appreciation of her gifts and powers which that prince of dramatists, actors, and good fellows had displayed. 'So encouraging,' she said, 'and so delightful, to find a person really above the jealousy which had hitherto led to her being so unjustly treated.'

After all, the faculty for discovering and utilising the powers of others to hit the public taste was the great secret of the great actor.

Miss Montressor did not know whether Bryan Duval had been quite so judicious and wise in the selection of certain other members of the company whom he proposed to take with him; she had her doubts on that point; but one must only work with the materials one has at hand. His fair Clara, in the character of critic and practical philosopher, afforded Mr. Dolby not a little amusement; and as he was not easily or often amused, he encouraged her to talk much more than usual. Mr. Dolby was not very communicative, nor did he, as a rule, like much talking—a defect in his disposition by no means agreeable to Miss Montressor's taste. He was rather given to absence of mind, and that is a tendency much disliked and resented by women, not unnaturally. Sometimes Mr. Dolby would fall into fits of musing, under whose influence he would rise and pace the room slowly to and fro, to and fro, with an utter abstraction in his face, which told Miss Montressor that his mind was far away, and that she was utterly banished from it, that she had no place at all, not even as a speck on the horizon, in his mental vision.

During these fits of abstraction he did not talk to himself aloud, indeed, but his lips moved; and his knitted brows, and the inward look of his eyes, were plain indications that he was not merely absent in the direct sense of idle purposeless reverie, but that some subject of deep, concentrated, and all-absorbing interest was occupying all the approaches to the citadel of thought.

Miss Montressor regarded this kind of thing as tiresome, a bore, and a mistake, a serious drawback to Mr. Dolby's excellence as a companion; but it inspired her with no further feeling, it wakened no curiosity. Business was almost as occult a phrase for Miss Montressor as it was for Helen Griswold, and she invariably concluded either that something had gone wrong in business or that Mr. Dolby was meditating some coup in business when he forgot to listen to her, left off talking to her, and walked up and down her pretty drawing-room, touching the chairs and tables unconsciously as he passed them with his finger tips, as she remembered having heard some one say Dr. Johnson used to touch the posts in Fleet-street.

Miss Montressor would have been seriously annoyed, however, if Mr. Dolby had gone off into one of his fits of absence on the present occasion. Her own business was in the wind now, and she considered it worthy of his undivided attention. He did not try her patience on this point; he listened with genuine interest, which received a quite perceptible stimulus when Miss Montressor mentioned that all the arrangements and preparations were being greatly assisted and facilitated by her American friend, Mr. Foster.

'Foster!' said Mr. Dolby, stooping to pick up his paper-knife; 'the New York man, I suppose?'

'Yes, I think so; a very pleasant agreeable man, and very fond of theatricals. He saw Bryan Duval years ago in New York, and called on him as soon as he came to London. He gave me a delightful sketch of the reception we are certain to meet with, and has promised us private introductions to no end.'

'Foster!' repeated Mr. Dolby, in a pondering tone. 'I don't think I know any one of the name—it is not common among us. What sort of looking man is he?'

'Decidedly good-looking—more like an Englishman than an American, I fancy, according to our notions of what you call the " American type." '

Mr. Dolby laughed. 'Don't talk stuff about the American type, my child; there is no such thing. There are scores of types among us, the most cosmopolitan and practical nation in the world. I now remember exactly what you mean by Mr. Foster's being more like an Englishman than an American. You mean that he looks healthy, cheery, and as if neither his sleep nor his digestion was ever troubled by overwork and anxiety. This is one of the favourite delusions of superficial writers and random talkers. Nothing has struck me, since I have been in London, more forcibly than the absence of the so-called English type among Englishmen. The rosy complexions, the stalwart forms, the unembarrassed open countenances, are just as scarce in London city as in New York; everybody looks anxious, it seems to me, and most people look tired. What is Foster?'

He asked the question with a strange suddenness. One would have thought by his manner he had forgotten Miss Montressor's mention of her friend in the discussion of the abstract question; but he had not.

'What is he? I don't know; I did not hear; but I presume he is over here on business of some kind. O, yes, by the bye, he must be, for Bryan Duval told me Mr.

Foster had come against his will, and wants to get back. That doesn't look like pleasure, does it?'

'Not particularly. However, Mr. Foster is no concern of mine, only your meeting any New York man reminds me to impress upon you that you must not talk about me. Are you attending to me, Clara?'

'O, yes, I am attending to you; and I am sure you need not be afraid of my telling anything you don't want to have known. I have kept you dark everywhere, and it is rather dull, I can tell you.'

'Rather dull, is it?' said Mr. Dolby, with a smile. 'You would like a little more dash about our cosy little arrangements, wouldn't you? You would like me to do the dinner-at-Richmond and drag-to-races business. Mr. Foster has been putting that into your head. No, no, my dear, that is not my line at all; and you must take me as I am, you know. You are going to star it besides, and you will have plenty of fun and frolic when

away from me; and I am all alone by myself in this big place.'

Miss Montressor gave her head a toss,
half disdainful, half incredulous. She remembered the ease with which Mr. Dolby
had made her acquaintance, and she believed in his constancy as little as she valued it.

'I shall not inquire too minutely into
your sources of consolation,' she said; 'and
if I were discontented with the present
state of things, you may be quite certain
that I should let you know it. It is only
men's wives, remember, who have to put
up with the style of life they don't like, because their husbands do like it; as for us,
Vive la liberté!'

'By all means,' said Mr. Dolby. 'I echo
the sentiment which you have declaimed so
prettily.'

She had advanced her right foot, tossed
her arm over her upreared head, and made
believe to wave a flag with a gesture full of

spirit. She often produced effects in private life of which her stage performances fell very far short.

'And since you have mentioned dinners at Richmond,' said Miss Montressor, with characteristic inconsequence, 'I may as well tell you at first as last that I am going to dine at Richmond with Duval and the whole lot. It is Mr. Foster's dinner, and he has sent me an invite through Duval, so I said I should be delighted. Duval drives me down—he is to call for me at four.'

She spoke with considerable volubility, which Mr. Dolby correctly interpreted.

'All right,' he replied; 'have we not just agreed *Vive la liberté?* and especially the *liberté* which brings such pleasant things in its train by its prolonged life. I am particularly grateful to my hospitable compatriot with a taste for theatricals, for I am obliged to go to Brighton to-morrow, and I shall not get back until Monday morning.'

'I was just about to tell you I should

not see you again till then, so it all hap-
pens most conveniently. He doesn't like
it a bit,' thought Miss Montressor, 'but he
carries it off pretty well—rather a clever
invention, that Brighton business; but it
doesn't impose on me.' She remarked aloud
simultaneously, with great good humour,
'This is really fortunate, as it turns out;
but you might have come, you know, if
you hadn't any objection to meeting Mr.
Foster—Bryan Duval would have got an
invite for you directly.'

'Thanks,' said Mr. Dolby, with perfect
gravity; 'such a kindness would have been
invaluable under other circumstances; but,
as you have just said, I have no fancy for
meeting Mr. Foster.'

'That is lucky,' thought Miss Montressor, as Mr. Dolby bade her adieu, 'for I
have.'

CHAPTER IX.

A DINNER OF CELEBRITIES.

MR. DUVAL, punctual to his appointment, pulled up the spanking chestnuts on to their haunches at Miss Montressor's door exactly at four o'clock on Sunday afternoon. They were very spanking chestnuts indeed, and the mail-phaeton glistened with varnish, and on every place on the harness where it was possible massive pieces of silver-plate had been put. All this was, of course, exaggerated and *outré*, and quite foreign to Bryan Duval's good taste; but that good taste had been swamped by a long connection with theatricals, and the wondering stares of the public, which he would formerly have shrunk from, he now took delight in, and disdained no method by which they might be attracted.

The phaeton, the horses, and the harness; the huge bearskin rug, with the French viscount's coronet, in red, elaborately displayed in one corner of it, which enwrapped his legs; the very costume of Mr. Duval himself, far more French than English, in its curly-brimmed hat, its brilliant necktie, its small jean boots with glittering tips, and its faultless *peau de Suède* gloves—all these were merely so many component parts of the general advertisement.

When people stopped in the street and nudged each other, muttering, as he could plainly see by the motion of their lips, 'That's Bryan Duval!' the actor - author inwardly winked, chuckling at the notoriety, and recognising the success of the performance—inwardly only, for he knew what a mistake it would have been to do away with the mysterious interest with which he was regarded by dropping into the comedian or buffoon, and therefore, when any public eye was on him, his face preserved the look of suffering earnestness which it was accustomed to wear on the stage.

When the garden-gate was opened, at the ring of the very elaborate groom who had slid himself into the road before the horses stopped, Miss Montressor appeared at the inner door of the villa ; and very pretty and picturesque she looked in her velvet skirt, and her upper dress of fine gray cloth velvet, bound and buttoned, and her small *chic* bonnet to match.

'How good of you to be so punctual!' she said, with a bright smile.

'And how noble of you to be ready at the appointed time!' he cried, from the phaeton. 'I will give you two extra sobs in your next tragic part as a reward.'

'You are a horror,' she said, shaking her handsome parasol at him, 'to speak of your own genius in that way—won't you come in?'

'No, thanks,' said Bryan, with a smile, which was so peculiar that Miss Montressor flushed slightly, and said in reply:

'There is no one here.'

'O, I don't mean that,' said Duval; 'and I should not have minded in the least if there had been; but we may as well take advantage of the brightness of the day, and have a stroll in Richmond - park before dinner.'

'O, that will be delightful!' said Miss Montressor. 'I am perfectly ready to start at once. Justine, have I got everything?'

Justine, who was really Jane Clark, but who had adopted her present appellation from the name of a soubrette in a melodrama, replied in the affirmative, and Miss Montressor having taken her place by Bryan's side, they drove away.

The wind was cool, but there was a bright sun, and the road was enlivened with crowds of people making the most of this, the first day of anything like fine weather, to escape from the dark streets to which they had been so long confined. They were off to the river-side public-houses of Putney and Mortlake, where they would talk over the details of the race between Oxford and Cambridge, which had recently been decided, or to the gardens of Kew, where they would pant in the tropical houses, and examine with intense interest the prospects of the budding trees and shrubs. They were pleasure-going people for the most part, who were accustomed to rank the theatre as one of their chief amusements, and who, from their hard benches in the pit, made a point of seeing any play which had a successful run at least once. So that Bryan Duval was well known by sight to most of them, as well as to the omnibus drivers, who would lean back, and roar in a hoarse voice behind their wash-leather gloves to the conductor: 'Know him? Dooval, the hactor!'

It is not to be supposed that Mr. Duval

was unmindful of the sensation he caused. When the omnibus men touched their hats to him, he raised his own with a grave graceful bow; but even when he spoke to his companion he still preserved the same impressive look upon his face.

'You see, Clara, my dear,' he said, with easy familiarity, though his lips never relaxed one whit, 'you see how very effective this is. People often ask me why I keep a mail-phaeton, and a brougham, and these chestnuts, and all the rest of it; they wonder I don't go about in a hansom cab; they say I should be much more independent, and it would be so much cheaper; but independently of the fact that I prefer my own handsome phaeton and comfortable brougham to any hansom cab, I find that the expense of them is almost met by the purposes they serve as an advertisement. Now this drive to-day is worth to me considerably more than a half column over the clock in the *Times*. These people would glance at that—they wouldn't read it; they never do read long advertisements—and forget all about it the next minute; but when they go home to-night, they will say to the children who are sitting up for them, or to the old man for whom it was too long a walk, "Who do you think we saw to-day? Why, Dooval, the performer — him that makes love so well—and driving such a swell trap!" and then one or the other of them will say they haven't seen me on the stage for some time, and wonder what I am doing, or what new piece I have written; and then they will look out the advertisement in the weekly paper, and you may take your oath that the money for a couple of hundred pit seats is as good as in my pocket at present.'

As they turned into Richmond-park they saw approaching them, by another road, a well-appointed drag, with four splendid roan horses, and driven by a tall gentlemanly-looking man, with a wonderfully woe-be-

gone countenance.   On the box beside him
sat an over - dressed young person with
blonde hair, and a face that was blue in the
sun and streaky in the shade.   She was
talking volubly to her companion, but none
of her sallies seemed to have the slightest
effect in rousing him.

'That's Laxington,' said Duval, as the
two vehicles neared each other, 'and Patty
Calvert by his side, of course.   You know
Laxington, don't you? Ah, then don't be
surprised if the bow which he gives you is
a very cool one; it is as much as his life is
worth to take notice of any other woman
when the fair Patty is by him.   He is too
much of a gentleman not to be courteous to
everybody, but my idea is, that he has a
very bad time of it.   And now just look at
those fellows on the top of the drag.   Two
or three of them can trace their descent
back to the Conqueror—though they would
have no pull over me there; there is no
better blood than that of the Duvals in all

France, my dear Clara, though that, per-haps, does not interest you—and the rest are the sons of fellows who have made their money by brewing, or mining, or carrying goods by railway, or some other gentle-manly occupation of the same kind, and yet there is not a ghost of an idea among the whole lot! I assure you, beyond telling a broad story and retailing the gossip of the backstairs, they have not a word to say for themselves. Dining in their company is the hardest work I know—harder even than it must be for you to listen to the odorifer-ous protestations of Mr. Hedger's Romeo.'

'I can fancy it,' she said, 'from my lit-tle experience in that line. But,' she added, looking saucily up at him, 'what do you do it for? I am always seeing your name in the papers as dining with swells—if you dislike it so, why do you do it?'

'As a matter of business, my dear,' said he, bending down, and speaking to her quietly, 'because the Duvals lost all their

property in the first revolution, and because
the beautiful estate of Knochnabocklish,
County Tipperary, which belonged to my
mother's family, was long since sold in the
Encumbered Estates Court; because I have
my own way to fight in the world, and to
do that, I must take whatever weapon
comes ready to my hand.   Do you imagine
that I like going to these dinners ? Do you
think I don't know the terms on which I
am received—as a superior Jack Pudding,
a table buffoon, a breaker of that dead dull
silence, which without me, or some one
equivalent to me, would reign unrelieved
throughout the whole dreary banquet? By
Jove, when the thought comes over me
sometimes, I am ready to start up and rush
out of the place, I am so ashamed of myself
for having descended to such depths;' and
Mr. Duval sent his whip curling over the
heads of the chestnuts, causing them to
plunge and dart off into a mad gallop.

Miss Montressor neither felt nor showed

the smallest fear. Had Lord Laxington or any of his friends been her charioteer on the occasion, she might possibly have speedily arranged an impromptu little scene; but she knew that any such device would be thrown away upon Bryan Duval, so she merely said:

'How a burst of passion suits you! You look remarkably well when you are in a rage.'

'Thanks, generous stranger,' said Bryan, conscious that the deer were his sole audience, and therefore permitting himself to lapse into a grin. 'It is ages since I have let out in that way, and it will be ages before I do so again. Thank Heaven, we shall have none of that sort to-day. Foster left the invitations in my hands, and I think I have got together rather a good party.'

As he spoke, they drew up to the door of the Star and Garter. Patricians as well as plebeians had taken advantage of the brightness of the day; there was a goodly show of drags and private carriages, from which the horses had been removed, and the hall was filled with persons who had either just arrived, or who were waiting for other members of their party. The groom was moving slowly off with the spanking chestnuts, and Bryan Duval, with Miss Montressor on his arm, was just ascending the steps, when a gentleman, separating himself from a knot of persons with whom he had been in conversation, advanced towards him —a man about the middle height, and a little under middle age, with a thick dark moustache and frank honest eyes.

'What, Foster, arrived already?' cried Bryan Duval. 'This is delightful. You know Miss Montressor, I believe?'

'Miss Montressor's reputation was familiar to me before I left my own country,' said Mr. Foster, raising his hat, 'and *I* have had the pleasure of becoming personally acquainted with her since my arrival here.'

'Very prettily said, Foster,' said Bryan Duval, as they shook hands. 'We came down early, in order that we might have a stroll in the park before dinner, and get an appetite for all your good things.'

'That's just what I proposed myself,' said Mr. Foster. 'I was naming it to our friends when you drew up. Let's join them, and all go together.'

They passed through the house into the garden, where some ten or a dozen people were gathered together on the lawn. There, in a loose brown overcoat, with heavy fur collar and cuffs, bell-crowned hat, fashionably-cut trousers, and patent-leather boots, was Pierrefonds, the celebrated dramatist, the man who had first introduced burlesques to the English stage—not the music-hall and breakdown ribaldry of the present day, but a combination of polished verse, of Attic wit, and French allusion which, some years ago, had made the fortunes of the Parthenon Theatre, and mainly helped to establish the great reputation of Madame Vaurien, its directress. Pierrefonds's bodily strength is not so great as in those days; his back is a little bowed, and his walk is somewhat shaky; but he is as quick-brained in his work, and as clever at tongue fence, as when the public thronged the pit to roar at his puns, and the brightest spirits of the day gathered in the greenroom to revel in his repartee.

The heavily-built, heavy-browed man in the dark-red beard, dressed in a suit of dark gray, with his hands in villanous mauvecoloured gloves, clasped behind his back, is Bob Spate, whose sparkling little comedies have in the last few years made the fortune of the little Imperial Theatre, and who is, perhaps, at the present time the most popular dramatist in England. He is a sad man, sparing of his speech and more sparing of his smile, giving one the idea either of being fond of solitude, or unaccustomed to and uncomfortable in the style of company in which he found himself. People who did not know his story wondered at such a successful man, wondered how one on whom the world's favour shone so brightly could be so melancholy, almost so morose.

They did not know that years ago, when the Imperial Theatre was called ' Higg's Hall of Amusement,' Bob Spate, then a young man, had written several of the comedies which had since so entranced the world, and had hawked them about here and there to London and provincial managers, always receiving them back upon his hands with a half civil, half contemptuous refusal. How was he, they argued, who was only a fifth-rate actor at a pound a week, to be able to write a comedy, or even, could he do so, what benefit could they reap by the production of the work of an unknown man ? So Bob Spate struggled and struggled in poverty, in sickness, and ofttimes in hunger; struggled on, and saw his wife die, and his children shrunken and wan and ailing, with the bitter knowledge that what he had written was better than nine-tenths of what he saw so highly paid for, but with the conviction that Fate was against him.

When bright little Lotty Bennett made her first attempt at establishing herself in life, and taking the dirty old Higg's Hall, changed it into the bright Imperial, she thought that as she herself was new in management, and she had a new company of actors, she might try a new author; and remembering Bob Spate, who had been an old friend of hers, and in whose energy and talent she had always faith, produced one of his comedies on her opening night. The success was immense, and from that time Bob Spate's fortune was made; wealth is his now, and honour, and such position as he chooses to take. What are they to him? Can they bring back to him the wife of his youth, whom he saw die by his side, not from actual starvation, indeed, but from lack of such necessaries as her delicate condition required? Can they efface from his mind the privations suffered by his children and himself? Can they bring back to him the youthful energy, the sanguine hope, the bright happy view of life so long since fled? I trow not. It is no wonder to me that Bob Spate is grave and reticent.

Anything but grave and reticent, however, is the gentleman standing next to him. Mr. Orlando Bounce is the youngest of elderly gentlemen, the brightest, cheeriest, emptiest rattletrap who for a half century has been acting light lovers and dashing roués, and who, if rumour is to be believed, has, during the same period, played the very same parts in private life. Old-fashioned is a sad epithet, but it is really applicable to Mr. Orlando Bounce; the peculiar roll of his blue-black hair, the peculiar side-cock of his shiny hat, his swinging gait, the elaborate motions of his arms—all these are essentially old-fashioned;

and when he bends in his back, and throws out his right arm and right leg with studied grace, you are reminded of Charles Surface, Captain Absolute, and all the riotous, swaggering young heroes of the comedies of those days. Before the arrival of Miss Montressor he has been paying great attention to the two ladies between whom he was standing, but they neither of them seemed to be much impressed by his attention. 'Get along, 'Lando, you are always talking such stuff,' is what one of them says to him. These are Rose and Blanche Wogsby, daughters of old Wogsby, manager of the northern circuit, and prime favourites in London. There is an extraordinary difference in their appearance: Blanche is very fair, with light-blue eyes and delicate skin, and a pretty bud of a mouth; Rose is tall and angular and swarthy, with dark hair, a strong jaw, and an underhanging lip—Blanche is a fool, Rose a remarkably clever girl. 'Blanche Wogsby is a fool,' frankly remarks Mr.

Wuff, the great theatrical impresario, 'but she is always safe for a dozen stalls a night from the young fellows who are spoony about her; but when it comes to the question of the tear-and-tatters fakement, when you want the real grit and no mistake about it, you must go to Rose. She will turn out a regular Rachel, you may depend upon it!' Mr. Wuff pronounced this word like the name of the lady who refused to be comforted, but meant to allude to the great French actress.

All present, both ladies and gentlemen, were, or seemed to be, greatly delighted at the new arrival. Bryan Duval was a general favourite. He was so kind and good-natured, so ready to lend any of his colleagues a helping hand, that they even forgave him his success. Miss Montressor was popular too, considering her prettiness and the position she had won for herself, more especially popular just at this moment, for the news of her American engagement had got wind, and it was felt that she would be out of all competitors' way for some time to come.

When the first greetings were over, Bryan Duval proposed that they should stroll towards the park, and thither they all repaired; Mr. Foster offering his arm to Miss Montressor, and remaining at some little distance behind the others.

'Do you know,' said he, 'that I am really very glad to have made your acquaintance—no, no,' he added quickly, as she looked up in his face and smiled rather maliciously; 'when I say so, it is not the ordinary compliment which you evidently imagine it to be. When you know me better, you will find I am not given to paying compliments, and that I invariably mean what I say.'

'I am glad to hear it in this case, at all events,' said Miss Montressor, with a little bow.

'It is the case,' he said. 'I felt interested in you long before I saw you. The fact is, Miss Montressor, I am a very busy man, far more immersed in business, environed by it, and tied down to it, than any of the gentlemen whom I have met here, and who are called your " City men," and when I am at home in New York the one relaxation I allow myself is the theatre.'

This man was a new experience to Miss Montressor, so far more earnest and dignified than the usual run of her associates. She tried to fall into his vein, and said quietly:

'I can understand its being a great resource to you.'

'It is a great relief,' he replied, 'in enabling me to throw off, for a time at least, the dull cares and worries, and to fill my mind with pictures and stories sufficiently absorbing to prevent its straying to Wallstreet and its ties. I have the pleasure of acquaintance with Mr. Leonard Serbski; you have heard of him?'

'Certainly,' said Miss Montressor; 'he

is the son of old James Serbski, who was so great in the *Bandit*, and whose portrait hangs in all the theatrical printshops, is he not?'

'The same,' replied Mr. Foster; 'a very handsome and gentlemanly fellow, and a very good actor. He has heard of you too, not merely through the medium of the English theatrical newspapers, but from people who have seen you, and has more than once mentioned your name to me.'

Miss Montressor was delighted with the compliment, under which she purred like a cat.

'I had no idea,' she said, raising her eyebrows, and throwing an expression of childish incredulity, which she knew was very becoming, into her face—'I had no idea that anybody in America had ever heard of poor little me; I thought I was going out there entirely unknown, and that I should have great difficulty in making my way.'

'You will find that you have happily

deceived yourself,' said Mr. Foster, with a smile. 'You will find that we Americans have a much livelier and deeper interest in all matters appertaining to literature and art than our more sober cousins on this side the Atlantic, that all artists of any reputation are known to us, and that when they come to our shores, they may be certain of a right hearty welcome.'

'I am very glad to hear you say so,' said Miss Montressor; 'and I only wish— it is a selfish thing to say, is it not?—that chance had sent you back to New York before our arrival, that I might be certain of having at least one personal friend.'

'It would have delighted me to have been of service to you, and perhaps I may even yet have the opportunity. When do you sail?'

'I think Mr. Duval mentioned the Cuba as the name of the vessel in which our passage was engaged.'

'The Cuba!' repeated Mr. Foster. 'I

am almost afraid that I shall be unable to get back by her, although I have made such progress in the business which brought me over here—business, you see, again, Miss Montressor—that I think it will not be necessary for me to remain in England so long as I at first anticipated.'

'If you were a married man, Mr. Foster, that would, I imagine, be very pleasant news to some one who is, what you call, "on the other side."'

'*If I were a married man!*' he exclaimed, with a laugh. 'Why, do you mean to say, Miss Montressor, that you have any doubt on the subject.'

'Well, you certainly have what I may call a family look about you,' she said, casting a careless glance over him; 'but as I have never heard you mention your wife, I concluded you were a bachelor.'

'I take it as a compliment,' he said, with another laugh, but this time more nervously and more seriously than before, 'or rather as a credit to myself, that even in the two short interviews which we have had since I made your acquaintance, I have not said something about my wife. It is the humour of most of my friends in New York to say that—excepting business matters, of course, where I never permit any domestic thoughts to intrude—that Helen's name is scarcely ever out of my mouth.'

'And quite right too,' said Miss Montressor. 'I detest a man who is married and ashamed of it, and who, when away from home, goes about, as it were, sailing under false colours. And so Mrs. Foster is called Helen? It is a very pretty name.'

'And she is a very pretty woman,' said Foster enthusiastically ; 'and not merely that, but the best and dearest little woman in the world. Here,' he added, plunging his hands into his waistcoat-pocket, and taking out from thence his watch, 'here is her portrait.' As he spoke, he placed the watch in Miss Montressor's hand.

Miss Montressor took the watch, and looked at its back, which was merely of engine-turned gold; then she pressed her fingers all round in search of some hidden spring, but finding none, shook her head blankly, and gave it back to her companion.

'I can see no portrait,' she said half pettishly.

'Of course not,' said he, with a laugh. 'You would not have me carry such a treasure as that for every one to see whenever I wanted to know the time. There,' he added, as the spring flew back and revealed the miniature, 'now you see my darling.'

'What a sweet face!' cried Miss Montressor, clapping her hands; 'so soft and pensive and loving! I don't wonder at your being fond of her, Mr. Foster, or being anxious to get back to her.'

'She is all that you say,' cried Mr. Foster, 'and more, God bless her!'

'It is quite refreshing, in these times of

separation and divorce courts, and all that sort of thing,' said Miss Montressor, 'to find such regular spooniness existing between a married couple. But if you are so fond of each other, why on earth didn't you bring her with you?'

'Didn't I tell you that I came over here on business, and that I never allowed even Helen to interfere with me when I am so engaged? Besides, she could not leave the child, which is indeed,' said Mr. Foster, 'the sweetest and most engaging—'

'Yes,' interrupted Miss Montressor; 'you may spare your rhapsodies about him, or her, or it. I don't go in for babies.'

'I am sure you would feel interested in her, if you only saw it; not merely is she the prettiest, tiniest mite, but she would move your sympathy for her bad health.'

'It has bad health, has it?' asked Miss Montressor carelessly.

'Very bad,' replied Foster. 'My wife's strength is scarcely equal to the discharge of her maternal duties, and she has had to engage a wet-nurse for the little one.'

'I hate wet-nurses,' said Miss Montressor shortly.

'They are not generally very trustworthy,' said Foster, 'but from a letter I have here' (producing one from his breast-pocket, and opening it), 'we seem to have found an exceptional treasure. Helen writes me in the strongest terms of the respectability of Mrs. Jenkins.'

'Mrs. Jenkins?' replied Miss Montressor, pricking up her ears. 'Who is she?'

'The wet-nurse of whom I have just spoken to you. You ought to have a kindly feeling towards her, for Helen tells me that she is an Englishwoman, and married to an Englishman for some time settled in New York.'

An instantaneous gloom spread over Miss Montressor's face, and she walked on by her companion's side in silence. Mrs. Jenkins? The name was common enough among English people, and yet a horrible feeling of fear crept over the young woman who chose to call herself Clara Montressor —a feeling of fear lest this Mrs. Jenkins, now occupying the situation of wet-nurse in Mr. Foster's family, should be none other than her own sister Bess.

She had not heard from Bess for months, but the last letter was dated from New York, and spoke of the shifty, hand-to-mouth existence which she and her husband were leading. Could it be possible that they could have fallen so low, that poverty could have come upon them so rapidly, as to induce her to undertake such a menial position? Was her husband dead? could he have deserted her? or what was the cause of her sudden collapse?

The more she thought over this matter, the more angry and impatient she grew; and Mr. Foster, noticing her preoccupation, thought it best not to attempt to renew the conversation just then.

Did ever anything happen so unfortunately? At any other time it would not have mattered in the least. Between Bess Jenkins, the wet-nurse in New York, and Clara Montressor, the theatrical star in London, there was a great gulf fixed; but when the theatrical star shifted its orbit to the city where her humble relation was living, the latter would naturally and undoubtedly proclaim to the world the family tie existing between them, and endeavour to make the most of it to aid her fallen fortune.

What should she do? what should she do? The saturnine face of Mr. Dolby rose before her mind in a minute. How should she treat him in regard to this matter? Certainly not tell him, for more reasons than one. He would be the last man in the world from whom she would receive any sympathy, and, besides, she does not choose to let him know the fact of the relationship. Towards him, then, she would preserve absolute silence; and a little further reflection decided her that her best plan was to wait, become better acquainted with Mr. Foster, and if she found him the good and honest man which, from her slight acquaintance with him, she fancied him to be—for even with her associates, and her experience of the world, she still believed in goodness and honesty—perhaps tell him the truth, and get his help in suppressing it. Yes, that was the course she would take; and having determined on it, she put the subject aside, and looked up at her companion, as though to say she were ready to renew the conversation.

'How pensive you have been!' said Foster earnestly. 'I did not like to break in upon your reverie.'

'I am very much obliged to you for leaving me to myself for those few moments,' she said, with a laugh; 'it doesn't sound complimentary, but it is true. You see, I am about to take what may be a rather serious step in my life, for if I succeed in America, my career is certain, and if I fail it may be wrecked, not merely there, but here; ill news travels apace, and it would soon be known that the London star had made a fiasco.'

'Even then, former experiences prove that your compatriots would retain their opinion of their favourite, and decline to accept our verdict,' said Mr. Foster. 'However, you need not be under any apprehensions of the sort; as I have told you before, you are sure to succeed.'

'I have great faith in Bryan Duval,' said Miss Montressor, 'and full reliance upon his generalship—he is popular too in New York, I understand.'

'Very popular indeed,' said Mr. Foster; 'he has achieved what is rather difficult there, a society reputation. This reputation he apparently wants to extend, for he has asked me for an introduction to my wife.'

'And you have given it to him?'

'Well, no,' said Mr. Foster, rather confusedly. 'There are—there are some reasons why I could not do so conveniently—in writing, I mean. Of course, I should be only too glad that both he and you should know Mrs.—Mrs. Foster, but I prefer waiting to introduce you personally on my arrival in New York; in case I cannot, there is yet a chance of my leaving by the same steamer. I see the others are making for the hotel, and I suppose, in my capacity of host, I ought to be the first there.'

It was a very good dinner, and went off remarkably well. In addition to the company already named, there were present Mr. Wuff, the celebrated manager of the Great National Theatre, who was supposed to be devoted to the legitimate drama, and where the performances at present consisted in a short farce, followed by a long 'oriental spectacular burlesque,' introducing horses, elephants, camels, and dancing women; Viscount Koolese, who was supposed to be ruining himself for Mademoi-

selle Petitpois, who brought with him his
friend Captain Clinker, the well-known gentleman rider, who said nothing, but whenever he was amused hissed loudly through
his teeth as though he were cleaning a
horse; a sound which seemed very unpleasant to the theatrical people present. There
was another manager too—Mr. Hodgkinson
of the Varieties—who kept up a running
fire of argument throughout the dinner
with Bryan Duval; the actor-author, whether he believed in it or not, maintaining
that the drama should be the school of
poetry and refinement, and that all the
theatrical managers should be made with
a view to that end—sentiments which Mr.
Hodgkinson violently pooh-poohed, declaring that his chief aim was to give whatever amusement paid the best.

'Let 'em have it,' said Mr. Hodgkinson,
who prided himself on being an eminently
practical man, striking his fist upon the
table; 'dogs and monkeys, Shakespeare, the

" Perfect Cure," Tom Mugger in four farces a night; or old Bounce here as Charles Surface, and all the rest of the Sheridan fakement—and the public is always wanting one or other of them, and my notion is, give them all a turn.'

Mr. Foster had placed Miss Montressor on his right hand, and though there was, of course, no opportunity and no occasion for returning to the subjects which they had touched upon in the park, he kept up a constant conversation with her. When the party was about breaking up, he proposed that she should return to town in his Victoria, where, as the night was somewhat cold, she would be warmer and more comfortable than in Bryan Duval's phaeton. Miss Montressor gladly accepted the offer, and, of course, Mr. Duval made no difficulty. He would, he thought, propose to drive Blanche Wogsby home, and take the opportunity of finding out whether she was really such a fool as she looked, or whether there would be any use in writing a part for her.

So the party broke up and the guests dispersed, and Bryan Duval, in taking farewell of Miss Montressor, told her that if the letters which he expected in the morning arrived, he should be able to let her know for certain the day of sailing for New York.

'It has been a delightful day, Mr. Foster,' said the actress, as they drove homewards, 'and I have enjoyed it immensely. Will you be able to give us any such outings in America?'

'I hope many such,' said Mr. Foster; 'but unless you take more care of yourself, I fear you will not be there to enjoy them. Seriously, your English spring weather is proverbially treacherous, and the wind tonight has a touch of east in it, which should induce you to wrap your shawl more closely round you.'

'I want to wrap myself up,' said Miss Montressor, justly estimating the truth of his words, 'for I am particularly susceptible to cold, but I cannot for this bothering pin.'

'What is the matter with the pin?' said Mr. Foster, laughing.

'It is not half strong enough to hold the shawl together. I cannot imagine how Justine sent me out with such a stupid thing.'

'Perhaps this will prove more effectual?' said Mr. Foster, taking the breast-pin from his cravat and offering it to her.

'Thanks very much,' she cried, accepting it with great readiness. 'What a very pretty pin! I love these cameos, and this is such a good-looking boy, with a straight nose and a queer cap on his head.'

'A Phrygian cap,' said Mr. Foster, laughing. 'It is a head of Ganymede. I had it set as a pin, I thought it so handsome.'

'Do you mean to say you brought it with you from Phrygia, or wherever it is?' asked the actress, who was vague in her geography.

'No, no,' said Mr. Foster, laughing still

more; 'but it was a sleeve-link when I first found it among my clothes when I opened my portmanteau in London. I suppose it belonged to my wife, as she is fond of such things, and that it was put up with my things by accident.'

The shawl comfortably pinned round her, Miss Montressor settled herself down to her corner, and neither she nor her companion spoke much more, being occupied with their own reflections. But when Mr. Foster took leave of her, he reminded her of Bryan Duval's last words, and told her that if he were prevented from sailing in the Cuba, he should certainly accompany the theatrical party down to Liverpool, and take leave of them on board.

Miss Montressor had been in very good spirits all day, notwithstanding the annoyance which, as we have seen, one portion of Mr. Foster's communication had caused her. She was agreeably conscious that her looks had been at their best. She was sufficiently refined, more by nature than by education, to recognise a gentleman when she met one, and to enjoy the ease and security conveyed by association with gentlemen. Mr. Foster had struck her from the first as a gentleman; not very brilliant indeed, but kind, courteous, and considerate—the sort of man who did not make women uncomfortable by either his looks or his language—and Miss Montressor appreciated this. She did not belong in the least to the reckless class among her order, and she had an almost morbid longing to be treated like a lady, as she expressed it, without the stately flattery on the one hand, or the freedom and easiness of the other, which ordinarily characterises the manner of the men with whom she habitually associated, and which were just as equally distasteful to her. Mr. Foster had gratified this longing; he had treated her with all the courtesy which he could have extended to the highest social position, and with a confidential fearlessness that had gone to the heart of the woman, who had always been poor in friends. When the pleasant day came to an end, Miss Montressor entered her pretty little house with a light step and a light heart, notwithstanding a vexation about Bess. By this time she had come to think of some means of getting over what would turn up. The day had seemed very short, and yet almost every minute of it had been full of pleasure. She was a little tired—those long pleasant days do tire one, after all—but she was not so cross as usual when, the feverishness of amusement having passed away, she returned to the home enlivened by no kindred presence. She answered her maid cheerfully, as the girl tripped down to the garden-gate at the summons of the bell, and let her mistress in.

'Yes, thank you, Justine, I am all right—rather tired; but we have had a delightful day.'

Justine removed the dainty bonnet and

the filmy lace mantle, folded the absurd parasol, which looked like a summer cabbage on a stalk, so flounced and furbelowed was the little silken dummy utterly useless as a sunshade, and while her mistress undid the buttons of her silver-gray silk gown, fetched a white morning robe, in which she clothed her tall full form. During these preliminary operations of her night toilette Miss Montressor talked away gaily — not about the day's proceedings, but about numerous trifles connected with her approaching journey and her sojourn in America. But when her hair had been brushed and the maid's duties were nearly completed, a trifling circumstance occurred which disturbed Miss Montressor's serenity. Her draped dressing-table stood in front of the large window of her bedroom, a French window opening to the floor, and looking out upon the trim little grassy terrace which ran along the back of the house, and from whence the garden, very pretty and effective for its extent, was reached by two steps. On this dressing - table stood her tolerably well-stored jewel-box. Miss Montressor was replacing some ornaments she had worn that day in the satin-lined tray of the casket when she perceived that the window was open, and asked Justine angrily whether she had been aware of this.

'No,' Justine replied; 'she hadn't noticed it.'

'Then you ought to have noticed it,' said Miss Montressor; 'such carelessness is abominable. Any one who pleased might have taken my jewel-box off the table without the least difficulty. The idea of leaving the window open on a Sunday, with no one in the house but yourself and such a lot of tramps about!'

Justine stood convicted, and could only promise that she would be more careful for the future; she was rather saucy sometimes, and ready with an answer to a rebuke, but on this occasion she said very little. There had been no one about the place, and though she had been the only person in the house —the cook and the page having had a holi-day—she had hardly left Miss Montressor's room, had indeed been reading at the open window the greater part of the day. But Justine, after her mistress was in bed, while folding up the shawl she had worn that day in so preoccupied a mood that she did not observe the pin with the carved gem for its head which was stuck into the soft woollen fabric, remembered, with a great sense of relief for the escaped danger, how there had come to the house late in the afternoon a man in the dress of a sailor who spoke like an American. This man had been rather hard to get rid of. He had pertina-ciously pressed his claim for a little assist-ance, and had been hard to persuade that the lady was not really at home. 'Just fancy,' thought Justine, 'if he had slunk round to the back of the house and seen the window open, and made off with the jewel-case; and I only wonder he didn't get hold of that or of something, for he was as objectionable a tramp as ever I saw.'

But that she had ever seen this objectionable tramp before, or heard his voice in any other capacity, Justine was totally unconscious; of which testimony to the efficacy of the change of costume the man in the sailor's dress was complacently aware. If Justine's quick eyes were deceived, it would deceive those of other people. A preliminary risk had been successfully run, and the omen was good.

CHAPTER X.

ON the day following the dinner at Richmond, Mr. Dolby presented himself at Miss
Montressor's abode somewhat later than she
had looked for his coming.

He did not find the fair lady in a very
serene mood—she was tired ; several small
domestic occurrences had ruffled her temper—which, to say the truth, was not a bad
one—during the early part of the day, and
when they met there was in the manner of
both those latent symptoms of ill-humour
which arise so often between persons in the
habit of being much in each other's society,
and who have, therefore, cast off the self-
restraint which occasionally tends to hypo-

crisy, but has, nevertheless, a wholesome influence in human intercourse.

Mr. Dolby omitted to tell Miss Montressor that she was looking beautiful—and
that was a grave offence. He, moreover,
omitted to exhibit any very lively curiosity
as to the proceedings of the previous day,
and though Miss Montressor did not care a
straw where he had passed the interval between their last and their present meeting,
or would not think of troubling herself to
make an inquiry about his proceedings, she
was not prepared to find him equally philo-
sophical.

'I suppose you forgot all about the
Richmond dinner?' she said to him, when a
few phrases, of course, had passed between
them.

'O no, I didn't forget it,' he said, 'but
I suppose one dinner at Richmond resem-
bles another very much, except in point of
talk. People eat the same things, drink
the same things, wear the same things, and

get intensely bored earlier or later in the evening, such as the case may be.'

'It was considerably later last evening,' replied Miss Montressor, with an aggravating smile, which, however, failed to aggravate Mr. Dolby, or to tempt him into an inquiry as to the vivifying principle of the previous day's entertainment. A more acute observer than Miss Montressor might have discerned in Mr. Dolby's manner preoccupation rather than indifference; but she was not an acute observer, and she was so honestly and unaffectedly interested in herself, and not interested in other people, that she resented his indifference. It would never have occurred to this woman—who, after all, was simple-minded—that any one who came to see her could think of anything but her, at least during the visit; and she therefore promptly resolved to punish Mr. Dolby for his departure from the laws laid down by her code of what was due to her. He did not seem inclined to take up the challenge she had flung down to him, and she found herself obliged to put an aggressive question.

'I suppose you don't care to know about the party yesterday,' she said, 'because it's quite clear I enjoyed myself, though you were not there; and men always resent that, though they can get away from us and be as jolly as possible.'

'My dear girl,' said Mr. Dolby, taking the inevitable photograph-book off the table, and carefully opening its ormolu clasps, as if the investigation of its contents offered to him a mental prospect of the most charming description, 'your theories about men are utterly absurd! I have told you so more than once, and I am not disposed to discuss the subject. I am very glad you had a pleasant day at Richmond, and— though I don't care for *réchauffés* in general, and you told me on Saturday who was to be there and all about it—I really didn't suppose you had any new or startling details to communicate. However, I don't at all mind hearing about the day if you are disposed to tell me. What did you wear ? who did you go with ? was the wine good ? what hour did you get back ?'

He had spoken in a monotonous tone of voice, with his eyes cast down, and turning over the clicking leaves of the photograph-book with one finger. Miss Montressor snatched it out of his hand with a suddenness which obliged him to look up, and he saw in her face that she was downright angry, which he had not intended her to be at this stage of the proceedings. A little later anger would be a wholesome senti-ment, which he proposed to awaken; so he smiled, took her hand, and said, with an attempted playfulness:

'Come—come, Clara, let us be friends; we're both a little bit out of sorts. I don't know what cause you may have; probably nothing more serious than your day yester-day having been too pleasant and having lasted too long. By the bye, what hour did you get back?'

'O, it was very late,' said Miss Montressor, withdrawing her hand, but not captiously, and arranging her bracelets. 'It was, in fact, awfully late, and Justine had got into the horrors under the influence of a solitary Sunday, and was full of possible robbers and tramps with a taste for murder; so I went to bed in rather an ill-temper, and several things which have happened to-day have not improved me. I have not seen you so disagreeable for an age; what's wrong?'

'I am excessively disappointed, Clara, and I am afraid you will be so too; but it cannot be helped. I find I shall not be able to go with you to Liverpool.'

'Not able to go with me to Liverpool, after promising that you would?' said Miss Montressor, with a good deal of vehemence. 'I never heard such a thing. That's really too bad, and I'm quite certain there is no real reason for it. I never knew you to be prevented doing a thing that you really cared to do. You are throwing me over, sir.'

'I am not throwing you over,' said Mr. Dolby coolly, 'and your suspicions are equally unjust to me and uncomplimentary to yourself. I told you I should see you off, and I not only wished to do so, but did not foresee the slightest difficulty about it; the difficulty has arisen, however. There is a man coming from New York whom I must see, and I can only see him on this day week, the day you leave.'

'How did you know?' said she quickly. 'There is no mail in.'

'And you never heard of the Atlantic cable, I suppose? A message cabled this morning, my child; and though I am your slave, you know, I have troublesome business for my second master, whom I am obliged to serve, and this time his claims are paramount. Don't get angry—don't

spoil the last few hours we shall have together for some time by causeless pique and
silly petulance—that sort of thing does not
attract me, and you don't look handsome
when you are out of temper. I would go
if I could. I cannot go, and there's an end
of it.'

'Please keep your comments on my
temper to yourself,' said Miss Montressor,
with an air of steady and determined ill-
humour, which, as Mr. Dolby had truly
remarked, did not become her. Like all
under-bred women, she could not venture
on anger; that most disfiguring of passions
was destructive to her dignity. She stood
up, brought both hands resolutely down
upon the table before her, and said, with a
slight stamp of her foot:

'It is not business that prevents you,
and I don't believe a word of it; it is because you are afraid of being seen with me.
You have always been playing a game of
hide-and-seek—you are no better than other

people, and I am no worse, and I hate such
hypocrisy. Who are you keeping up a character for, or with, a character that is to
suffer because you are civil to an actress,
who was going by herself to the other side
of the world? I suppose you think there
is more chance of your being seen in Liverpool than London by some "goody"
acquaintance, who would be excessively
shocked.'

'Please don't talk in that tone, Clara.
It's rather shocking—though I don't expect
you to understand why. However, I don't
mind telling you that you are not altogether wrong, though you put my objection
to being seen with your pleasant associates
on a totally mistaken footing; and as I don't
like to part with you in a fit of offence, I
shall take the trouble of explaining to you
again that it is a matter of great importance
to me not to be seen at present by any
New York people, and not to have my
name mentioned in the hearing of such. I

have told you that the business I am engaged upon in London might be seriously
compromised by manœuvring friends from
the other side, that my whole fortune is involved in it—an argument whose strength
you might very fairly comprehend, though,
mind, I do not mean to say you are as mer-
cenary as most women, or more expensive
than others; but after all, a very little imprudence on your part, you see, might make
a considerable difference to you, and all the
difference to me. The truth is, I have the
appointment in London I have told you of,
and I could not go down to Liverpool and
run the risk of being seen there by the set
who I am advised are coming from New
York by the mail that will arrive just before the Cuba goes out; so now you know
all about it. You will take my word, won't
you, that I am very sorry; and you will
take that frown off your face, for I really
want to talk to you seriously, and this is
childish, however pretty.'

Miss Montressor was endowed with very good sense, and it showed her at once that Dolby was speaking the truth.   She did not understand much about his business— she had never cared enough about him to try;—but she was alive to the reasonableness of his refusal to gratify her wish—a wish dictated a good deal more by *amour propre* than any sentimental longing to enjoy his society to the last possible moment.   She accordingly recovered herself; and with no more protest than a dubious shake of the head, resumed her seat and prepared to listen to Mr. Dolby.

'Well,' she said, 'go on; what have you got to say to me?'

'That,' said Mr. Dolby seriously, ' I have always found you trustworthy.   Nine women out of ten, on being told that it was a matter of importance to me that no American in London should know that I am in London, would have betrayed the fact to every American of her acquaintance, from an amiable desire to penetrate the motive of my injunction. I am quite sure that you have scrupulously observed it.'

'Certainly,' said she; 'it don't matter to me. Why should I go and talk about you when you ask me not? That would be simply perverse.'

'Nine women out of ten, my dear,' said Mr. Dolby, 'are perverse. I esteem myself very fortunate to have found the exceptional tenth.'

'I hate men who are always sneering at women,' said Miss Montressor; 'it's a bad sign.'

'For the women?'

'No, sir, for the men. But I daresay you have been very ill-treated in your time; only it doesn't matter to me what women you think ill of, provided you think well of me, so I will take the compliment. I assure you once again that I never mentioned your name to any American—or rather, I should say, to the only American I know.

'That is Mr. Foster,' said Mr. Dolby, with a slight effort.

'Yes,' said Miss Montressor, 'to Mr. Foster. I like him so much,' she added in a brisk parenthesis. 'Do you know him?'

'No,' said Mr. Dolby; 'never heard of him. What's his business?'

'O, I am sure I don't know. You don't suppose he talked of business yesterday, or would bother me about it under any circumstances. He was much too jolly for that. I hate your concentrated men who cannot think of anything but money-making, and cannot talk of anything except the way they make it.'

'You like the money though,' said Dolby.

'O yes, I like the money; but I like it as a result, just as one likes dinner. Dinner would be a nuisance if one had to see it cooked and know how it is done; so would money if one had to superintend the getting of it. Mr. Foster never alludes to business.'

'Ah, well,' said Mr. Dolby, 'that is no proof that he may not be in something that would clash with me, and it is highly important that he should not know of my existence,—here at least. Was there any one with him yesterday?'

'No; he came alone—I mean not with Duval and me in the mail phaeton—and was the life of the evening—such a charming man!'

'Married?' asked Mr. Dolby.

'Yes, married; and to a charming wife, if one may judge by the way he talked about her.'

'What wretched taste!' said Mr. Dolby. 'You hate a man who talks about business. I hate a man who talks about domesticities. I go so far with the Orientals as this, that men should not talk about their womankind or suffer them to be mentioned to them in general, except by very intimate friends, who ought to be mutual.'

'How do you know that we are not

NO NONSENSE ABOUT HER.   261

very intimate friends?' said Miss Montressor, suddenly assuming an air of coquettishness. The serious tone of the interview had been unduly prolonged for her taste, and she had no capacity for ethics.

'It must be a very sudden intimacy if it exists,' said Mr. Dolby angrily.

'I didn't say it was not; one doesn't take a lifetime to like a man, to find it out, and let him know the fact.'

'No,' said Mr. Dolby, 'one doesn't; nor does he take a lifetime to reciprocate, even though he has this charming wife, and talks the most arrant nonsense about her.'

'Mr. Foster talks no nonsense,' said Miss Montressor, 'about her or about me, which is what you mean to imply. He made himself exceedingly agreeable—shall I tell you how?' (There was a sudden depth in her voice and a sudden depth in her eyes which would have had pathetic meaning to any one capable of reading it.)

'You don't answer; well, then, I will. By treating me exactly like a lady, with the respect he might have paid to his wife or his sister, and without the smallest intimation, except when I turned the conversation in that direction, that he remembered that I was only an actress.'

'Pooh!' said Dolby, in a tone of exaggerated contempt, and watching her closely as he spoke; 'that is the stalest trick. A man gets introduced to you because you are an actress simply, and ingratiates himself with you by pretending to forget it. You ought to be too sharp to be done by such an artifice as that, and have too much respect for your profession to be pleased by it. After all, my dear, what's your claim to consideration and admiration? First, that you are a pretty woman, which is always the first claim that any woman can have; secondly, that you are a popular actress. When a man atttempts to put either admiration or consideration on any other footing, he is in reality flattering you with an additional assumption that you are a fool. I was more honest than your new admirer, Miss Montressor.'

'My new admirer, as you choose to call him, Mr. Dolby, is at least more courteous than you are. I heard him tell Duval, to whom he does not speak on business matters, that he would postpone an important one, for the purpose of accompanying us to Liverpool.'

Mr. Dolby drew a long breath, and his nostrils expanded slowly—a symptom of emotion with which Miss Montressor was acquainted.

'I have roused him now in earnest,' she said to herself; 'we shall have a storm.'

But she either misinterpreted the source of this manifestation, or Mr. Dolby exhibited great self-control. Instead of the passion with which she expected to be rebuked, he simply replied, leaning back indolently in his chair, and clasping his hands

over his head, with an air of absolute leisure, 'Lucky dog who can postpone business for pleasure.'

'He regards it as a very great pleasure,
I assure you, Mr. Dolby. He said he would
not lose the last sight of us for any consideration, and deeply regretted his absence
from New York during our stay.'

'Of course he introduced you to his
charming wife.'

'Not just yet—not by letter, I mean.
He hopes to be able to return before our
engagement terminates; and to have, as he
expressed it, "the pleasure of making the
introduction in person."'

Mr. Dolby laughed an exceedingly inso-
lent laugh.

'And you believe that?'

'Yes,' she said. 'Don't you?'

'Certainly not. I believe he has not
the slightest intention that you should know
his wife—it might not be convenient; he
might not have quite so strong an opinion

of your discretion as I have—he has not had so much time to found one, you know—and circumstances may defeat his hope of getting back during your stay. I don't think you will make Mrs. Foster's acquaintance, but I suppose you will find Mr. Foster waiting to receive you at Liverpool on your return.'

'He says so,' she answered, 'if he does not come to New York. It is all very well your sneering at a man you know nothing about, but I believe in Mr. Foster, and you shall not sneer me out of it.'

'I have no wish to interfere with your faith in him or in time,' said Mr. Dolby; 'but with reference to this same coming back, have you anything to say about me?'

Miss Montressor blushed violently. The cold cynicism of his tone hurt her. She was not sensitive, and she did not care about him, but she was proud in her way, and he had offended her.

'I do not understand your meaning,'

she said. 'I do not know what you are driving at.'

'Not at an enigma, my dear. I do not want you to go away with any notion of acting a little private drama in addition to those in which I have no doubt you will make a stunning success in my country. You know well enough what a matter-of-fact fellow I am, how entirely averse to acting off the boards. I am not jealous, it is too much trouble, and I like to leave people as much freedom of action as I claim for myself; still I like things on the square, you know; and it strikes me very forcibly that it might suit your book to put our future relations upon a tolerably liberal footing.'

'Do you mean to say you want to get rid of me?' said Miss Montressor, surprised for the moment out of her coquetry into very real disgust.

'Certainly not; but, unless I am very much mistaken, it might be convenient to you to be aware that you can get rid of me, without any manœuvring on the subject, without making an enemy of me, and without incurring any grave risk of breaking my heart.'

'I don't believe you have any heart to break,' said she.

'O yes, I have; quite as much as is convenient to myself, or pleasant for you. Look here, Clara, there is a long parting before us—at all events, a parting you have chosen to make, in the interests of your professional career. I think you are quite right, and I don't want to hamper your action with any consideration for the future. When you return, I shall be very glad to see you, but you can choose for yourself, without any reproach from me, whatever may be the end of your choice, the exact character of our future relations. You can take them up at their present point, if you please; you can reduce them to simple friendship. I don't believe in platonics, remember, as a starting-point, but I believe in them as a terminus. You know where I am always to be heard of. I presume I shall hear from you during your stay in America, but if it bores you to write, I shall not tie you to a correspondence; on your return to England, any communication you may choose to make to me shall, as we say in business, "receive my prompt consideration." '

With these words Mr. Dolby rose, buttoned his coat, took up his hat and gloves, and offered Miss Montressor his hand, with the cool ease of an ordinary morning visitor. She was so thoroughly taken aback by his demeanour, that for once in her life nature and training alike failed her. She was entirely unequal to the emergency, so she stood perfectly still and perfectly silent, without making any movement in answer to the gesture by which he invited her to shake hands. In another instant Mr. Dolby had left the room, and she heard him walk quietly down-stairs and out of the house, before she recovered herself.

For a good hour Miss Montressor sat in her drawing-room, under the impression of this extraordinary parting scene. It was a demonstration not only unlike but entirely opposed to anything which she had previously remarked in Mr. Dolby's character. If this woman had been naturally very clever—or had learned by education to decipher the relations between cause and effect, as they are. indicated by the actions of human beings—she would probably have hit upon the truth; she would probably have discerned that Mr. Dolby had for the nonce assumed her profession, that she had seen him in the character of an actor, performing a part as carefully rehearsed as any that she had ever played, and with far more serious meaning.

During her confused meditations it had crossed her mind vaguely that there might be a motive for his extraordinary conduct;

for the senseless outburst of jealousy which, though he strenuously denied it, his line of action betrayed.

'What can he mean by it?' she asked herself a score of times, something within her heart contending with the natural and somewhat flattering interpretation which she placed upon his behaviour. She remembered his ill-humour when they first met, and it flashed across her mind as a possibility that he might have come with the predetermination to quarrel with her. But why? She had given him no offence, their last interview had been conducted on the footing of a perfectly good understanding; and the mention of Mr. Foster, to which his present freak manifestly referred, had only arisen on the present occasion.

Miss Montressor was lost in a maze; but among its bewilderments love had no place, as she was quite conscious that she could be perfectly happy without Mr. Dolby, could it be proved that he had made up his mind to do without her. And she was not vehemently impatient to emerge from the maze.

The cogitation of an hour ended, after all, in the contented conviction on her part that the sole motive of Mr. Dolby's conduct was jealousy, mingled with a perception that he was a stronger-willed and worse-tempered man than she had hitherto believed him to be.

The practical conclusion at which she arrived was that she would leave Mr. Dolby to himself for a day or two. He had spoken of 'faith in time,' and though Miss Montressor was not apt in poetry, she was capable of prosaic adaptation of the adage. She would try the effect of time at very little cost to herself. It was a matter of comparative indifference whether she saw Mr. Dolby the next day, or the next day but one, or the next day but two; he should have a wholesome interval to come to his senses, and she really had a great deal to do in preparing for her voyage to America.

Within an hour and a half after Mr. Dolby's precipitate exit from Miss Montressor's abode, that lady was engaged in the prosaic occupation of making out, with Justine's assistance, an inventory of the finery which, apart from her stage wardrobe, she considered it necessary to take to New York; then an inventory of that which she was leaving behind. These grave matters of business were of sufficient importance to shroud in temporary oblivion anything so insignificant as a quarrel with Mr. Dolby—which might, perhaps, be called a lover's quarrel on his side, but which, to Miss Montressor, had simply the commonplace aspect of a fit of unqualified ill-temper.

'He is a surly brute!' was her summary; 'and I will just leave him to come out of his sulk.'

*　　*　　*　　*　　*

The next day but one went over, the first stage in the process of Mr. Dolby's coming to his senses in Miss Montressor's mental time-table. The hours did not drag; there was plenty to do, there were many people to see; and the more Miss Montressor dwelt upon the prospect of her Transatlantic trip, higher rose the hopes of reaching her ambition—the expectant star about to get a real opportunity of shining for the first time could not trouble her head with such mundane matters as a sullen admirer.

The next day but two went over, and Mr. Dolby neither came nor wrote. No conciliatory bouquet, no reconciliatory bracelet, came as a token of regret and repentance. Things were looking serious, and Miss Montressor was sorry—sorry, not with the interested annoyance of a woman of her class who has awakened to the fear of losing a rich lover, but sorry with a genuine kindheartedness, reluctant to part with an old friend on bad terms; and with something of the irresistible tenderness which all but a thoroughly heartless woman must feel towards one whose feelings she believes herself to have miscalculated and wounded unawares.

'Who could have thought,' she said to herself on the morning of the third day, 'that he cared about me so much?' A shallow generalisation; but somehow one would have liked Miss Montressor less if she had been more clear-sighted — if she had been able to read between the lines on this occasion.

At noon of the third day Miss Montressor took a resolution and a sheet of her very best note-paper, with a very dainty monogram in rose-colour and silver, and scrawled upon it just two of those characteristic lines which mean so much and say so little, which are full of apology without humiliating concession, and full of attraction without formal invitation.

This letter she despatched by her page, who returned considerably before she looked for him, bringing back the letter, with the unexpected intelligence that Mr. Dolby had left his lodgings at Queen-street, Mayfair, 'for good;' and also that the people at the house had no address and no instructions for the forwarding of communications intended for him.

Miss Montressor had literally never been so taken aback in all her life.

'What could it mean?' she again asked herself, this time without the vaguest indication of an answer; and now she was alarmed as well as sorry. Was this indeed to be a fatal and irreparable breach?

Rather late on the same evening a four-wheeled cab drove up at the door of No. 192 Queen-street, Mayfair. Two females occupied the vehicle, one of whom was presumably, by her dress and appearance, a respectable upper servant, perhaps a lady's-maid. Her dress was plain, but suitable to such an assumption, and she was closely veiled. Leaving her companion, who was somewhat similarly attired, in the cab, this person rang the bell and requested to see the mistress of the house. A respectable-looking middle-aged woman, with a countenance exhibiting that peculiar mixture of conventional complacency and ever-present anxiety which characterises the London lodging-house keeper, presented herself in answer to this request, and begged that the lady would step into her little room. The visitor explained at once, to avoid disappointing the expectation which was very plainly written in the landlady's anxious face, that she had not come to engage rooms, that she had merely called to make inquiry. This announcement was met with no decrease of civility, and the invitation to walk in was repeated.

It then appeared that the visitor had called to inquire about the lodger who had recently left No. 192, and the interview be-

tween the two women very rapidly assumed
the aspect of a gossiping chat. Mrs. Watts
was very sorry to part with her lodger,
'which he was quite the gentleman,' and
had gone away with his luggage in a cab,
and himself in a hansom. There was a deal
of luggage; them big boxes as come from
New York, and looks like ladies' boxes
mostly. Mrs. Watts could not say where
he had gone to—certainly she had seen the
labels; but they were two brass labels
slipped into the ticket grooves, with New
York in black letters upon the metal.

'Was there any name upon the trunks?'
asked the visitor.

Mrs. Watts was quite sure there was no
name anywhere, nor upon the strapped-up
package of railway rugs, canes, and um-
brellas.

'Did Mrs. Watts,' asked the visitor,
'entertain any doubt whatever upon the
subject?'

'He had left in the evening, and she

had heard the driver of the hansom directed to Euston Station, to catch the Liverpool mail.'

This was conclusive, and the visitor, taking a polite leave of Mrs. Watts, got into the cab and drove home without exchanging a single word with her companion.

'He is mad,' thought Miss Montressor during that silent drive, and there was a strange complacency in her mind at this conclusion—'he is stark mad with jealousy —who would have thought it? Well, he will get over it, I suppose, and it don't matter to me.'

A reader of Miss Montressor's thoughts and an observer of Miss Montressor's ways would have been struck by the extraordinary frequency with which that little phrase, 'it don't matter to me,' turned up in Miss Montressor's meditations, and found utterance in Miss Montressor's speech. 'It don't matter to me, but it is better than any play I ever had a part in, or any play I know anything about, for I firmly believe he has gone to New York beforehand to watch me.'

It was not, on the whole, an unnatural conclusion; it only lacked one element of probability. Mr. Dolby's unexpected access of jealousy had come on apropos of Mr. Foster. Mr. Foster was not gone nor going to New York. This circumstance struck Miss Montressor after some time, but she got over the little difficulty by reasoning from the particular to the general, and making up her mind that Mr. Dolby had suddenly arrived at the conclusion that she was not to be trusted either here or there. There was something flattering in this conclusion, even to a woman who did not care a straw about him, and who was in her way, and according to her light, frank and honest. Miss Montressor liked the flattery, accepted the conclusion, did not trouble herself to reconcile it with Mr. Dolby's story of his appointment in London, and supposed they should meet over there, and it would be all good fun.

*   *   *   *   *

Only one incident remains to be recorded with regard to Miss Montressor's visit to Mr. Dolby's former abode. It was not under that familiar name that she inquired for him; it was not in that name that Mrs. Watts praised the amiability, and lamented the departure of her late lodger, nor had that been the name inscribed upon the note with the rose-and-silver monogram.

END OF VOL. I.

LONDON :
ROBSON AND SONS, PRINTERS, PANCRAS ROAD, N.W.

www.ingramcontent.com/pod-product-compliance
Lightning Source LLC
Chambersburg PA
CBHW030629030726
47497CB00006B/1698